Previous Manny Rivera Mysteries by Rich Curtin:

Artifacts of Death
Manny Rivera Mystery #1

February's Files
Manny Rivera Mystery #2

Trails of Deception
Manny Rivera Mystery #3

MoonShadow Murder
Manny Rivera Mystery #4

Deadly Games
Manny Rivera Mystery #5

Author's Website:

www.richcurtinnovels.com

DEATH SAINT

A Manny Rivera Mystery

Rich Curtin

This is a work of fiction. Names, characters, places, and events are products of the author's imagination or are used fictitiously and are not to be construed as real. Any resemblance to actual incidents, locales, organizations, or persons, living or dead, is entirely coincidental.

ISBN: 1532925905
ISBN-13: 9781532925900
Library of Congress Control Number: 2016907267
CreateSpace Independent Publishing Platform
North Charleston, South Carolina

Printed in the United States of America

DEATH SAINT

1

IT WAS SUNDAY, a week before Easter, and Manny Rivera was in the office as part of a contingent of deputy sheriffs assigned extra duty during Moab's annual Jeep Safari. He was sitting at his desk sipping on a mug of black coffee, waiting for the phone to ring and hoping it wouldn't.

The Jeep Safari, a ten-day event during which Jeep owners from all over the country converged on southeast Utah to test their backcountry driving skills and the durability of their four-wheel-drive vehicles, was in full swing. Caravans of Jeeps attempted to navigate challenging trails with names like Hell's Revenge, Wipe Out Hill, and Metal Masher. During this testosterone-driven event, vehicle rollovers, injuries, situations requiring rescue, traffic accidents, bar fights, and theft were inevitable. Thus far, no serious problems had been reported—but Rivera knew it was just a matter of time.

The first call came at eleven o'clock in the morning. He put down his coffee and snatched the telephone out of its cradle. The caller was a nurse at the Moab Regional Hospital.

"Please hold, Deputy Rivera," she said. "Mrs. Foster, one of our patients, would like to speak with you. She says it's urgent."

Rivera heard some fumbling with the phone and what sounded like heavy breathing. "Deputy Rivera, this is Faye Foster. Please come to the hospital right away," she said in a weak, gasping voice. "I need to clear my conscience about something before I die."

Rivera hung up the phone, grabbed his Stetson, and rushed out of the office. He was sure this had nothing to do with the Jeep Safari. He knew Mrs. Foster had been ill but he had no idea she was near death. She was an elderly widow who lived in an old house on a few dozen acres out in Spanish Valley. He'd visited her home several times last year when she'd complained about a recurring theft of vegetables from her garden. It was jackrabbits, he knew then, but he also knew she was lonely after her husband had passed away and she just wanted someone to talk to.

He entered the hospital lobby, obtained Mrs. Foster's room number at the front desk, and headed down the hallway. He intercepted a nurse along the way, asked about Mrs. Foster's condition, and learned she had Stage IV emphysema.

"Mrs. Foster is seventy-six years old and she's been a smoker all of her adult life. Her lungs are barely functioning." The nurse lowered her voice to a whisper. "It's just a matter of time now, maybe a day or two."

Faye Foster lay in her bed under a sheet, eyes squeezed shut in a frown, looking small on the large mattress. Her craggy face was weathered and wrinkled, and her gray-brown hair appeared greasy and matted as though it hadn't been shampooed in weeks. An oxygen tube was clipped to her nose and her breathing was labored.

Rivera removed his hat. "Mrs. Foster," he said in a soft voice.

Her eyes opened. She squinted and blinked at Rivera as though trying to bring him into focus. Her eyebrows rose slightly upon recognizing him. She pushed down with her elbows and struggled to sit upright, but couldn't. She gave up and just lay there, managing a half smile which quickly faded. "Thanks for coming, Deputy Rivera. I need to tell you about something that happened a long time ago. It was fifteen years ago, almost to the day, but I remember it like it was yesterday." She stopped and took a series of short breaths. "It's been troubling my conscience all this time."

Rivera placed his hat on a table and extracted a pen and notebook from his shirt pocket.

"There was a young man killed up in the LaSal Mountains back then," she said. "He was shot in the chest. The sheriff never could figure out who he was or why he was killed." She stopped talking to catch her breath and pointed to a glass of water on the bedside table.

Rivera handed her the glass. Grasping it with trembling hands, she raised her head off the pillow and took a couple of sputtering sips. Rivera watched her drink, vaguely remembering hearing about the case. It had happened years before he'd arrived in Moab.

She pushed the glass toward him and he returned it to the table. Her intense, brown eyes stared past him at the far wall. "It always bothered me that since he was never identified, his family was never notified of his death. They're probably still wondering what happened to him. His mother must be heartbroken." She paused and took several breaths, the oxygen apparatus wheezing and clicking each time she inhaled. "My husband Wilford was hiking in the mountains that day and discovered the body. Instead of calling the authorities, the heartless old fool just stole the young man's backpack. It was new and Wilford wanted it, so he just unsnapped the straps, removed it from the body, and brought it home." She stopped again and struggled to catch her breath. "Later he made an anonymous call to the Sheriff's Office from a pay phone in town and reported the location of the body. The next day, he told me about what he'd done and I've been ashamed and troubled ever since."

Rivera understood the point. An item in the backpack might have revealed the man's identity. "What did your husband do with the contents of the backpack?"

"That's what I wanted to tell you. Wilford's dead and buried and I'm near gone, so it won't matter if it all comes out now." She swallowed and spoke with an urgent tone. "We have a barn on our property. There's a workshop in the rear for tools and things. Wilford dumped the contents of the backpack into one of the drawers in the workbench. I think it's all still there."

Rivera nodded and folded up his notepad. "I'll check it out."

She reached out, held his wrist weakly with her hand, and looked at him with pleading eyes. "Deputy Rivera, promise me you'll find his family and tell them what happened to their boy."

He patted her hand. "I promise."

2

RIVERA WONDERED IF he'd just made a promise he might not be able to keep. There was no guarantee the items from the backpack, even if they were still in the barn, would reveal the identity of the dead man.

He walked across the hospital parking lot to his white Ford F-150 pickup truck with the Grand County Sheriff's Office insignia emblazoned on the doors. He hoisted himself into the cab, pulled his iPhone from his pocket, and called Millie Ives, the sheriff's dispatcher. He summarized his conversation with Mrs. Foster and informed Millie he was heading for the Foster residence to search the barn.

"I think this might be too important to postpone," he said. "The rest of the department should be able to handle whatever problems arise with the Jeep Safari."

"I agree, Manny. Go ahead and check it out."

"I'm on my way." He started his engine and pulled out of the parking lot.

"I remember that case well," she said. Millie had been the sheriff's dispatcher for over thirty years. She knew the department's history better than anyone. "Leroy Bradshaw was sheriff back then—and fairly new at the job. He decided to handle the case himself. Clues at the scene led him to believe it was murder, but without knowing the victim's identity, he was never able to determine a motive for the killing or identify any suspects. It was the only case in his entire career that he'd been unable to solve. He was a proud man and, although he never mentioned it, I know it always bothered him."

"How come he handled the case himself?"

She laughed. "Well, Manny, at the risk of over-inflating your ego, until you hired on, Sheriff Bradshaw never had a deputy that was any good as an investigator. The sheriff himself was arguably one of the best in Utah, so back then he handled all the tough cases himself." She chuckled. "Then you came along."

Rivera appreciated the compliment but dodged it. "We may have to reopen that case."

"I think Sheriff Bradshaw would be real interested in hearing about whatever you find in that barn."

"If anything useful turns up, I'll give him a call."

As he drove, Rivera reflected on the four years he had worked for Sheriff Bradshaw. Rivera had known little about investigative work when he hired on as a deputy. Before coming to Moab, he'd been a city cop for four years in Las Cruces, the city where he was born and raised in the bosom of a tight-knit Hispanic family. Bradshaw had apparently seen something promising in Rivera and had taken him under his wing. He patiently taught Rivera the basics of investigative work, instructing him in the proper ways to gather facts, establish a precise chronology, apply logic, make inferences, and search for motives. Most of what Rivera now knew about conducting an effective investigation he'd learned from Bradshaw in those early days. He missed his old boss and mentor. What a crying shame such a fine man had been replaced by an incompetent blowhard like Rivera's current boss, Sheriff Denny Campbell.

Rivera drove south out of Moab toward the Foster residence, pondering the promise he'd made to Mrs. Foster. His motive had been to bring some measure of tranquility to a dying woman in her final days—it was the right thing to do. Now he hoped he'd be able to deliver on that promise.

He turned left off Spanish Valley Drive and drove down an asphalt road which dead ended at the Foster place. He continued across a cattle guard onto a gravel driveway. The Foster house was nestled among four large cottonwood trees, now bright green with spring foliage. The house was old, probably built in the early 1900s, and was constructed with red rock blocks. The driveway continued past the house and led to empty animal pens and an old barn, its maroon paint faded and peeling. Behind the barn, alfalfa fields which had gone to seed stretched out toward a majestic 400-foot high red rock bluff. Beyond that rose the LaSal Mountains.

He grabbed his flashlight, entered the barn, and found the workshop in a back corner. He swept away a jungle of cobwebs with his arm and stepped into the small room. A three-inch hole in the outside wall allowed a shaft of light to slant across the darkened space. As he entered, he heard the flutter of wings as a couple of panicked birds flew off from the nest they'd built next to the opening. He spotted a cord hanging from a single light bulb mounted on the ceiling. He pulled it, illuminating the workshop.

In the center of the room was an eight-foot long wooden workbench with a column of four built-in steel drawers at one end. It was ruggedly constructed with heavy beams and lag bolts, and looked to be at least fifty years old. An air compressor and battery charger sat atop the workbench, along with cans of lubricants and paints. Shovels, pitchforks, and picks were stacked in one corner of the room and rolls of garden hoses hung from hangers mounted on the wall. Nearby, a Kelty backpack hung on a hook. He took out his iPhone and photographed the room and its contents.

He pulled open the workbench drawers one at a time and inspected the contents. The top three drawers contained assorted hand tools and spare parts—nothing pertinent to his investigation. The bottom drawer was slightly ajar but stuck. With the help of leverage from a crowbar, he forced it open. He aimed his flashlight into the drawer, peered inside, and jumped back at the sight of a coiled rattlesnake. Further inspection and careful prodding with the crowbar revealed that the snake was dead—and had been for a long time. Rivera's hopes were lifted when his eyes fell on a compass and a folded map—this drawer had to be the place where Wilford Foster had dumped the contents of the backpack.

Rivera took a series of photographs, then pulled on a pair of latex gloves and began extracting the contents of the drawer, starting with the compass. It was a typical magnetic compass with a flip-open cover, the kind most hikers carried with them in the back-country. He blew off the dust, dropped it into a clear plastic evidence bag, and placed it on top of the bench. Next he removed the map, noting from its legend that it was a trail map of the LaSal Mountains. He would unfold it and inspect it back in his office where there was better light. He bagged it and placed it next to the compass. A six-by-eight-inch book with a worn, brown leatherette cover came next—it appeared to be some kind of personal journal. He blew the dust off, opened it, and saw the words *David Archuleta, Santa Elena, New Mexico* written on the inside of the front cover. Rivera felt himself relax a bit—now he'd be able to locate the victim's family and keep the promise he'd made to Mrs. Foster. And now he recognized that he had a new challenge—find out why Archuleta was killed in the LaSals fifteen years ago and by whom.

As a native of New Mexico, Rivera was very familiar with the geography of the state and the names and locations of most of its cities and towns—but he'd never heard of Santa Elena. He figured it had to be a small town in some remote area well off the beaten path.

He riffled through the pages of the journal. They were filled with notes, poems, sketches, and brief thoughts and observations about the backcountry. Some of the sketches were black and white, others were drawn in color. He would study the journal in more detail later, but his initial impression was that Archuleta was a thinking man and a lover of nature and the outdoors. He placed the journal in an evidence bag and set it on top of the workbench.

He continued extracting each item from the drawer, blowing off the dust, then inspecting and bagging it. There were assorted snacks, a small roll of toilet paper, a box of one-gallon Ziploc plastic bags, an unopened two-liter bottle of Aquafina water, a Swiss Army penknife, and a small flashlight. There was also a small statuette in the drawer. He held it with both hands and examined it, thinking how odd it was for a hiker to carry an item like this in his backpack. About six inches tall and made of a heavy resinous material, it was in the form of a skeletal figure clad in black and holding a scythe. It reminded Rivera of the Day of the

Dead figurines so popular in the Hispanic culture. He bagged it and added it to the pile.

In the bottom of the drawer, he found a leather wallet containing Archuleta's driver's license and a faded photograph. According to the license, Archuleta would have been twenty-three years old when he was killed. The photo showed a handsome Hispanic woman in her mid-forties with an intelligent, narrow face and high cheekbones. He turned it over—nothing was written on the back. Because Rivera always carried a picture of his own mother in his wallet, he figured the woman in the photo was probably Archuleta's mother. Also in the wallet were some soft drink discount coupons, a Miraculous Medal, and a mass card showing an image of the Virgin of Guadalupe.

Scattered in the bottom of the drawer were eight ballpoint pens, each a different color. He bagged them and made a final inspection of the drawer to make sure he hadn't missed anything. The only remaining items were some dead mealy bugs, a few spider webs, the desiccated carcass of a beetle, a couple of feathers, the dead rattlesnake, and a large spider cowering in the corner. Rivera took one last photograph of the drawer, gathered up the evidence including the Kelty backpack hanging on the wall, and returned to his vehicle.

As Rivera drove back to the office, his thoughts were on David Archuleta. A man who hiked the backcountry, wrote poetry, and sketched what he saw in nature didn't seem like the kind of person who would have enemies. Yet he was struck down in the prime of his life. Might Archuleta's death have simply been a hunting accident? According to Millie Ives, Leroy Bradshaw had reason to believe the shooting was deliberate. And Bradshaw was not the kind to misjudge such matters.

3

RIVERA DEPOSITED THE evidence from Wilford Foster's workbench on his desktop, then went to the file room and retrieved the case file on the shooting in the mountains. He detoured by the break room, refilled his mug with coffee, and returned to his office.

He took a sip and began contemplating the task before him. He was confident he could find Archuleta's family to inform them about their son's death, but what chance did he have of solving a fifteen-year-old murder case? He was aware that cold cases are solved on occasion because new evidence is discovered or because today's technology allows a new interpretation of old evidence, but it wasn't nearly as common as screenwriters of popular television shows would have viewers believe.

He leaned back in his chair, hoisted his feet onto his desk, and opened the case file. Leroy Bradshaw was listed as the investigating officer. An anonymous tip had been received by telephone stating that a dead man had been spotted in the LaSals near Haystack

Mountain. The caller, a male, had provided the GPS coordinates of the corpse. Bradshaw and Deputy Sheriff L.D. Mincey had gone to the scene to investigate. The victim, a Hispanic male, had been shot once in the chest with a .30 caliber bullet. He had long, dark brown hair, a goatee, and hazel eyes. He was five feet nine inches tall and weighed 150 pounds. No abandoned vehicle had been found in the area. The Medical Examiner estimated the victim was 23 or 24 years old. Curiously, he had long welt-like lesions on his back similar to those that would result from a whipping, except the scars were vertical instead of horizontal. The M.E. had been unable to suggest a possible cause for the scars.

The victim had been shot approximately five hours before the call came into the Sheriff's Office. There were no powder burns on his clothing so Bradshaw had surmised the shot had come from a rifle some distance away. The file contained a packet of photos showing the victim from several angles and the general area where his body had been discovered. No usable footprints had been found as the area was mostly sandstone cap rock. Bradshaw had noted in the file that the victim was found in a wide-open area where a hunting accident would have been highly improbable. The man was wearing a white windbreaker and would not have been mistaken for a mule deer or an elk. Furthermore, in areas near the crime scene where sandstone depressions were filled with blow sand, no fresh animal tracks could be found. These facts led Bradshaw to conclude the shooting was deliberate and not a hunting mishap. The file also stated that eighty dollars had been found in the victim's pocket, thereby ruling out robbery. Subsequent searches throughout Grand County and neighboring San Juan County for an abandoned vehicle that might have belonged to the victim had proven fruitless. Lastly, no one had filed a missing person report.

Rivera went to the evidence locker and examined the items which had been removed from the victim's body: clothing, boots, socks, a cap with a shaman figure embroidered on front, the cash, a few coins, and a handkerchief. The front of the shirt had dried blood stains and a hole where the bullet had torn through. An evidence bag contained the slug.

Rivera returned to his office, closed the door to discourage interruptions which might break his train of thought, and sat down. It was time to take a closer look at the journal which lay hidden for fifteen years in Foster's workbench. He opened the front cover and reread the name—*David Archuleta, Santa Elena, New Mexico.* Rivera turned to his computer and checked Archuleta for wants and warrants, finding none. He checked with the FBI's National Crime Information Center—no missing person matching that name had been reported. Next, he checked the maps in his New

Mexico atlas and learned that Santa Elena was a small village in northern New Mexico. It was located in Rio Arriba County at the foot of the Tusas Mountains. The atlas listed the population of Santa Elena at 306. No wonder he'd never heard of it.

The door to Rivera's office flew open and slammed against the wall. He looked up to behold Sheriff Denny Campbell, six-feet-four inches of incompetence dressed in a sheriff's uniform. His perpetual frown was fiercer than usual. "What's this I hear about you running for sheriff next year?" he boomed. His jaw jutted out and there was a trace of spittle on his lower lip.

Rivera was taken aback for an instant. First of all, he was surprised Campbell was in the office on a weekend. That was something he'd never seen before— Campbell spent most of his time on the golf course. And secondly, Rivera had no plans to run for sheriff.

"Where did you hear that, Sheriff?"

"Never mind where I heard it. Is it true?"

Rivera shrugged. "I've made no announcement that I was planning to run for sheriff," he said calmly. He could have simply informed Campbell it wasn't true but where's the fun in that? Campbell had been a pain in Rivera's butt ever since winning an uncontested election for sheriff, and each encounter with him seemed to be more and more unpleasant. Leroy Bradshaw had dropped his bid for re-election as sheriff after his wife Jill had died of cancer. *"Too many memories here,"* he'd said, and left town when his term was finished. Campbell had been the only other candidate running for sheriff at the time—as a result, he won the election.

"You can't be a deputy working for me and running for my office at the same time. It's unethical. It's disloyal," Campbell sputtered.

Loyalty is a two-way street, Rivera thought to himself. He smiled and turned his hands palms up. "I don't know where that came from, but I've said nothing to anyone about running for sheriff." Rivera suspected he knew the source. One of the county councilmen had approached him about a week ago and suggested he consider it. He'd said some of the other councilmen and many of Moab's citizens were getting fed up with Campbell's rudeness and arrogance, and were ready for a change. Rivera had listened politely, nodded, and told the councilman he hadn't considered running. And he hadn't. And wouldn't. He loved his job as an investigator—but he might as well keep Campbell guessing. Not that it would accomplish anything—but seeing Campbell squirm like this produced in Rivera a satisfying warmth in a passive-aggressive sort of way.

Campbell frowned. "I could fire you, you know."

Rivera was confident he wouldn't be fired. He was good at his job and popular in Moab. "I know, Sheriff. And I could resign." There was a long moment of silence as the two men stared at each other.

Campbell's eyes fell on Rivera's desk. He pointed. "What's all that stuff?" he asked, apparently ready for a change of subject.

"We just got a new lead on an old murder case. A man was shot and killed in the LaSals fifteen years ago. At the time, there was no way to identify him so the case was never solved. As of today, we have his identity. I need to go to New Mexico to follow up on it." He handed the case file to Campbell and explained the source of the new lead. Campbell skimmed through the file and handed it back.

"First of all, you need to arrest Mrs. Foster as an accessory after the fact. She withheld information in a murder case."

"No point. She's terminal," said Rivera.

"So? She committed a crime. Arrest her."

"According to the nurse, she'll be gone in a matter of days."

"I don't give a damn. She committed a felony and must be arrested. It'll send a message to everyone in the county that the laws must be respected by all. No exceptions." Campbell paused. "Or are you inventing your own laws again? I warned you about that."

Rivera knew he'd developed a reputation for bending the law when it conflicted with his personal value system. When he felt the circumstances warranted it, he would often look the other way. His grandfather, a wise man he respected more than anyone else, had helped

Rivera understand the tradeoff during the deputy's first murder case. *"Justice is more important than the letter of the law,"* he'd said, and Rivera had never forgotten that. Campbell, on the other hand, was a stickler for the letter of the law. "If she gets out of the hospital alive, I'll arrest her," said Rivera.

"See that you do. Where in New Mexico are you going?"

"Santa Elena. It's in Rio Arriba County on the Colorado border."

After asking a few irrelevant questions, Campbell looked at his watch and left. Rivera figured it was probably getting close to tee time. He shook his head, hoping someone competent and experienced would step up soon and announce a run for sheriff. Besides the county councilman, several important merchants in Moab had hinted strongly that Rivera should run. He knew it was probably the right thing to do for the community, but he wasn't sure he would enjoy it. Why change jobs when you love the kind of work you're doing?

Rivera closed his office door, took a sip of coffee, and forced himself to refocus on the Archuleta case. He'd sometimes detoured through Rio Arriba County on trips between Moab and Las Cruces to visit his family, but had spent time there only twice. Three years ago, he'd explored the Ghost Ranch where Georgia O'Keeffe had painted many of her stunning landscapes.

Then, a year later, he'd visited the village of Abiquiu, one of the oldest settlements in New Mexico. Other than those visits as a tourist, he knew little about the county.

He turned to his computer and searched for information on Rio Arriba County. The first thing that struck him was how sparsely populated it was. In an area larger than the state of Connecticut, it had a population of only 40,000. Sixty-three percent of the land was owned by the U.S. Forest Service and the U.S. Bureau of Land Management. Much of the privately-owned land was originally Spanish and Mexican land grants dating back centuries. The county seat was an unincorporated settlement called Tierra Amarilla with a population of about 1,000. He thought that was an odd fact and wondered how many counties in the entire country had county seats that were unincorporated. Probably not many.

Española, on the southeastern tip of the county, was the only city of any size—it had about 10,000 residents. Most of the remaining 29,000 people lived in isolated, backcountry settlements scattered throughout the county, many of them in the mountains. One of those settlements was Santa Elena. It was in the Tusas Mountains about twenty miles southeast of Tierra Amarilla at an elevation of 7,400 feet. The settlement's demographics indicated that 100% of the people living there spoke Spanish. He noted that the people didn't speak Spanish because they were immigrants—they spoke Spanish because most of the families traced their roots back to the territorial era of New Mexico and even earlier when New Mexico was still part of Mexico. Some went all the way back to the time of the Spanish Conquistadors.

Rivera checked Google Earth to get a bird's eye view of Santa Elena and zoomed in for a close inspection. The village was nestled in a high, narrow valley in the mountains. The main part of the town looked to be about four blocks long and two blocks wide and all of the buildings appeared to be residential. It was surrounded by grassland and cultivated fields dotted with a few homes and outbuildings. Beyond the fields, the surrounding terrain was mountainous forest land.

Rivera was becoming more and more curious about Rio Arriba County. He continued his search and learned that the county sheriff had recently been found guilty of charges stemming from the misuse of county funds, grand theft, extortion, and lying to a federal grand jury. He was now serving a fifteen-year prison term. An interim sheriff named Ruben Gallegos had been appointed by the county commissioners until a new election could be held. A couple of articles Rivera found indicated that Rio Arriba County had a reputation for lawlessness and drug abuse.

He took another sip of coffee and sat back, wondering what a young man from a small village in Rio

Arriba County was doing in the LaSal Mountains. The limited quantity of water and snacks in his backpack indicated he was on a day hike. The lack of a vehicle in the area belonging to the victim suggested someone had dropped Archuleta off at one of the trailheads. Rivera presumed that individual had planned to return and pick him up later in the day.

Rivera unfolded the map of the LaSal Mountains that Archuleta was carrying and spread it out on his desk. He examined every square inch of it with a large magnifying glass. It was a standard trail map available from several Moab merchants, but it lacked pen or pencil markings that might have indicated Archuleta's route or destination. He refolded it and turned his attention to the Kelty backpack, unzipping all the zippers and opening all the pockets. It was empty. The initials *D.A.* were inscribed on the inside of one of the flaps. Rivera wondered why Archuleta had carried his things in a full-size backpack instead of a lighter and less bulky daypack. The items Rivera had found in the barn would easily have fit into a daypack.

The big question that hung in Rivera's mind was why no one had reported Archuleta missing. The individual who had dropped him off in the LaSals should have become concerned when Archuleta hadn't shown up at the pickup point by the agreed-upon time. It was not an unusual occurrence in the canyon country for a hiker to get injured on the trail or lost in a maze of canyons, so standard procedures had long ago been established to deal with the problem. Normally, the person responsible for pick up would alert the sheriff immediately. The sheriff would notify the volunteers of Moab's Search and Rescue team and a search would be organized and conducted. But none of that had happened. Was it possible the person who had dropped Archuleta off in the mountains was the one who had killed him? Rivera thought about that for a long time. He could find no reason to rule it out.

Rivera began thumbing through the pages of Archuleta's journal. Archuleta had written down his thoughts and feelings about life and his wishes that the world would someday find peace and contentment. There were quotes from Jesus Christ, Mahatma Gandhi, Mother Teresa, and Martin Luther King Jr. Several pages contained poems of one or two stanzas written by Archuleta, some in Spanish, others in English. The poetry wasn't world class in Rivera's view, but it wasn't half bad. The subjects were wide ranging and included sunrises, sunsets, the forest, the night sky, desert wildflowers, cactus, bears, mountain lions, mule deer, and anthills. It was clear Archuleta was a lover of nature and the backcountry. Some of the poems with religious overtones had crucifixes drawn above them. Several pages in the journal contained hiking logs. Rivera studied them carefully, hoping to recognize a location, a landmark, or the name of a creek, mesa, or trail. But the logs had none of that, only what Archuleta had seen and felt and thought about during the course of his wanderings through the backcountry.

There were many sketches in the journal, some in black and white, others in color. The colors matched the ballpoint pens Rivera had found in Foster's workbench drawer. The drawings included things Archuleta likely had observed during his hikes: trees, plants, animals, arrowheads, potsherds, mushrooms, lichen-covered rocks, cactus, caves, arches, and geologic formations. Rivera pictured him taking a break from his hiking, sitting down in the soft grass, leaning back against a tree, and sketching what lay before him.

Rivera decided to make copies of Archuleta's drawings and give them to Amy Rousseau this evening. They had a date to meet at La Jacaranda for margaritas, Mexican food, and mariachi music. She'd said she had some great news to tell him. Amy was a PhD biologist Rivera had been dating for about eight months. With her scientific background, perhaps she or one of her associates at the Dolores River Research Institute might recognize something in the drawings that would shed light on Archuleta, his background, or what he was doing in the LaSals. Rivera knew that Amy always enjoyed helping him with his cases. It gave her a chance to apply her extensive knowledge of plant biology to real-world problems.

Rivera removed Archuleta's driver's license from his wallet and studied his photograph. He was lean and handsome and his facial expression was relaxed, sincere, and friendly. It was the face of a man in whose company one would immediately feel comfortable. For fifteen years, David Archuleta had been a nameless man in an unopened file folder. Now, as Rivera read the man's journal and learned about how he saw the world, it seemed as though he were coming to life—and Rivera was beginning to like him as a person.

Rivera saw nothing in the journal to suggest a motive for Archuleta's murder. Quite the opposite. He seemed like the kind of person everyone would want as a friend—a gentle soul who loved nature.

4

RIVERA DIALED THE Rio Arriba County Sheriff's Office and waited. After four rings, the cheerful voice of a young woman came on the line.

"Sheriff's Office, Ruby speaking. How may I help you?"

Rivera identified himself and asked to speak with the interim sheriff.

"One moment, please."

After an extended wait, a man came on the line. "You're a deputy from where?" The voice had undercurrents of unfriendliness.

"Grand County, Utah."

"What's this about?"

"Is this Sheriff Ruben Gallegos?"

"This is Deputy Sheriff Gilbert Jaramillo. State your business."

Rivera wasn't used to this kind of rudeness from a fellow peace officer. "I'm investigating a murder we had up here a while back and I'd like to talk to the sheriff about it. Get some help. Ask him a few questions."

There was a pause. "What kind of questions?"

Rivera detested bureaucracy even more than rudeness. He was still irritated after his encounter with Sheriff Campbell and reached the limit of his patience faster than usual. "Deputy, I'd like to speak with the sheriff. Is he there?"

"Well yeah, but I ..."

Rivera raised his voice. "Then put him on the line." He listened to a few seconds of Jaramillo's breathing.

"Hold on."

Rivera could hear two men talking in the background. He couldn't make out their words but the tone suggested they were arguing about something. Finally, a voice came on the line.

"This is Ruben Gallegos."

Rivera introduced himself and explained what had happened to David Archuleta fifteen years ago and the recent discovery of information pertinent to the case. He said he would like to stop by the sheriff's office for a visit tomorrow, then go to Santa Elena and give Archuleta's parents the bad news. He told Gallegos about the promise he'd made to a dying woman.

"Sure, Deputy, that's fine. C'mon down. Did you say Grand County, Utah?"

"Yes."

"Beautiful country. My wife and I visited Arches National Park about twenty years ago."

"There's a lot more to see up here than just Arches. If you ever get back this way, I'd be happy to show you some more of the sights. We're real proud of our red rock canyons."

"I may take you up on that someday. Anything else you need to do while you're down here?"

"Well, yes. After I inform Archuleta's family, I'll need to begin an investigation into his murder. His hometown would be a logical place to start asking questions."

"Well, uh, sure. I guess that's okay. What time do you expect to arrive?"

Rivera detected a subtle change in the sheriff's tone of voice—from friendly and cooperative to cautious and reticent. "Right after lunch, say one or one-thirty."

"Barring an emergency, I'll be here to meet you. And let me apologize for Deputy Jaramillo's rudeness. Ever since our former sheriff went to prison, he thinks he's in charge of the place. I think he's a little put off that I was selected as interim sheriff and he wasn't. He likes to throw his weight around. Have you spent much time in New Mexico?"

"I grew up in Las Cruces. I was a city cop there for four years."

"Well, you'll find that northern New Mexico is quite a bit different from what you're used to. People, especially the ones living in remote villages like Santa Elena, don't care for strangers coming around and asking questions." He cleared his throat. "They may not be real open to answering them. You speak Spanish?"

"Yes, I do."

"That's good because most of the people in those mountain villages don't speak English. Are you coming alone?"

"That's what I was planning."

"I'd suggest you bring backup, just in case. I'll assign a deputy to work with you but we're a little short-handed so my deputy can't be with you full-time. You best not be alone up in those villages. And make sure whoever you bring speaks Spanish."

"We're a little short-handed too. This is Jeep Safari week up here and the town is full of four-wheel drives and pumped-up over-achievers. It's a busy time for law enforcement so I'll have to come alone. Besides, I'm the only deputy we've got who speaks Spanish."

"Well, okay then. I'll see you tomorrow."

Rivera thanked him, said goodbye, and hung up the phone. He sat back in his chair, took a sip of coffee, and wondered what he was getting into. He thought he knew New Mexico, but Rio Arriba County sounded nothing like Las Cruces.

5

RIVERA SIPPED ON a margarita while he waited for Amy Rousseau at La Jacaranda, a popular Mexican restaurant on Main Street in downtown Moab. He was sitting at their favorite table in the far corner of the outdoor patio, enjoying his drink and munching on chips and salsa. Mariachi music wafted over the patio and the evening was cool.

Feathery bands of cirrus clouds in the western sky slowly transformed themselves into pink and purple brushstrokes across the horizon as the sun dropped out of sight behind the Moab Rim. The traffic on Main Street was picking up as people in dust-covered Jeeps returned to town after a day of backcountry adventure. A few of the vehicles had noticeable dents and scratches but the occupants seemed happy and unconcerned. Moab's watering holes and restaurants would be filling up fast.

He glanced at his watch—as usual, Amy was fifteen minutes late. He didn't mind at all, and he wasn't surprised. He'd gotten used to waiting. It wasn't just

Amy—he'd noticed that almost every woman he'd dated over the years was well practiced in the art of arriving late. He had a theory that women believed it just wouldn't look right if they arrived before the man—or even at the same time. Heaven forbid they should appear too eager. Rivera, a student of human nature, figured it was worldly wisdom handed down to young girls by their mothers. He smiled and took another sip of his margarita.

The tequila was beginning to produce a warm and pleasant numbness in Rivera's cheeks. He could feel the tension in his body dissipating and his mind beginning to relax. The irritation he felt as a result of Sheriff Campbell's paranoia and Deputy Jaramillo's macho rant was beginning to fade.

Rivera was looking forward to discussing the Archuleta matter with Amy, even though revealing the details of an ongoing investigation with a civilian was a violation of regulations. In Amy's case, the regulations made no sense. She was more of an expert consultant than an ordinary civilian, and he was certain he could count on her to keep the information confidential. She was smart and, several times in the past, she'd come up with insightful ideas that had helped him visualize his case from a different perspective. Besides, Rivera had decided years ago to treat police regulations more like suggestions than requirements.

Amy had said she'd be bringing some great news to share with him tonight. Perhaps another one of her peer-reviewed papers had been accepted for publication by an important biology journal. Or maybe she'd discovered a new species of plant in Hell Roaring Canyon where she'd recently been conducting a plant inventory. Whatever the reason, he was looking forward to spending the evening with her.

His thoughts reverted back to Sheriff Campbell and today's ridiculous dustup. Now relaxed, Rivera could think about the matter with more of a detached objectivity. He loved his work and his role in keeping Moab safe for residents and visitors, but he wasn't sure how much more of his overbearing boss he'd be willing to put up with. Moab needed a new sheriff, that was certain, but Rivera knew the job was not for him. Someone needed to unseat Campbell in the upcoming election. Rivera's mind churned through the possibilities of people who might be good candidates. There were several deputies who had enough law enforcement experience but who lacked the organizational skills necessary to do the job right. He considered Deputy Sheriff Dave Tibbetts, a man he knew had the brains and energy for the job, but he was too young and inexperienced.

Perhaps one of the cops in the Moab Police Department would be right for the job. He stepped through the possibilities in his mind but couldn't think of anyone who stood out. Of course, Denny Campbell would run for another term—and without opposition, he would win again. And that would be an intolerable outcome. Rivera felt like the world was conspiring to force him to run for sheriff against his will. If only Leroy Bradshaw would decide to return to Moab, the problem would be solved.

Rivera spotted Amy tiptoeing between the Jeeps with the grace of a ballerina as she crossed Main Street. She looked radiant and beautiful as ever. When she spotted him, her face lit up with a gorgeous smile. Amy was in her late twenties, five-feet-five-inches tall, with large hazel eyes and honey-colored hair with blonde highlights. The white slacks and yellow top she was wearing accentuated her tan. She came to the table, gave Rivera a hug and a peck on the lips, and sat down.

She grinned. "I see you started without me. Tough day today?"

He smiled. "Just the usual. Another unpleasant encounter with the sheriff. I needed this first margarita for medicinal purposes." He waved over the waiter and ordered a mango daiquiri for Amy and another margarita for himself.

Amy was eyeing the thick manila envelope beside the dish of salsa. "What's in the envelope?"

He picked it up and handed it to her. "These are for you. They're copies of drawings from a murdered man's journal. His body was found in the LaSal Mountains fifteen years ago." He told her about the call from Mrs. Foster and how he'd found the journal in the barn. "He was a pretty good artist. He seemed to enjoy drawing the things he encountered in the backcountry—plant life, rock formations, and so forth. Maybe you and your fellow scientists could take a look at them in the next day or two and tell me if any information about his background or activities can be gleaned from them. It's a long shot but right now any ideas or insights would be helpful."

She looked into the envelope and thumbed through the copies, scrutinizing each for a brief moment. "Are you looking for anything in particular?"

"Just insights into the man and his life. I'm not sure yet what I'm looking for."

She smiled. "Okay. I'll study these and then pass them around at the Institute. I'm sure my associates will come up with a lot of ideas, most of them probably more humorous than informative. They're all comedians."

"Anything would be helpful, even a good laugh."

"What have you learned about the murdered man so far?"

"Very little, except that he's from a small village in New Mexico called Santa Elena. It's in Rio Arriba County on the Colorado border. I'm leaving early to-morrow morning to meet with the sheriff down there and visit the victim's family."

The drinks arrived and they ordered dinner, a fish plate for her and chicken enchiladas with green sauce for him.

"You said you had some great news," said Rivera.

Amy shifted in her seat, looked at her drink. "I do."

"So tell me."

She produced a nervous smile. "You know my sabbatical at D.R.R.I. is about over and I've been applying for a teaching position at a few universities."

He nodded.

"Well, guess what. I've been offered a job as Assistant Professor at the University of New Mexico. I'll be able to continue my research there."

Rivera didn't like the sound of that. "Albuquerque?"

"Yes. Isn't that exciting?"

"Yes, but I was hoping you'd take a position at the Utah State University campus here in Moab."

"Oh, Manny. That's an extension school—just a few classrooms in a strip center. I need to be at a major university where I can continue my research and publish papers on my work. I want a place where I can collaborate with experienced research professors and mentor graduate students. My botany career means a lot to me. You know that."

Rivera felt his heart sinking. "Albuquerque is a long way from Moab."

"Manny, I'm not sure I could survive here. If I stayed in Moab, my career would stagnate and I'd suffocate professionally. I'd be miserable. Come with me, Manny. You can get a job in Albuquerque as a deputy or a policeman. Besides, you hate working for Sheriff Campbell. A change would do you good."

What had started out as an enjoyable dinner with Amy at their favorite restaurant on a beautiful evening had just turned unpleasant, disappointing, and stressful. Today was not Rivera's day. Amy's "great news" had turned out to be a bombshell. He promised her he would think it over.

6

BENTLEY, RIVERA'S LABRADOR RETRIEVER, had been moping around all morning as he usually did when Rivera was packing his suitcase for a trip. Rivera had made it clear that it wasn't possible for him to come along, so Bentley was now well into his beleaguered, heartbroken routine—walking from room to room with his head hung low, making a pathetic, whining sound designed to instill feelings of guilt in his thoughtless master.

"You'll be staying with the boys next door," said Rivera, stroking the dog on the head. "You remember, Robbie and Sonny. You like playing with them." Bentley perked up at the mention of their names and began wagging his tail.

Rivera had arranged for Bob and Margie Stickle, his dear friends and next-door neighbors, to feed the guppies in his ten-gallon aquarium and take care of Bentley during his absence. He left home at six o'clock in the morning, stopped at McDonalds to pick up a large coffee, and began the long drive to Tierra

Amarilla. Because of the early hour, there was little traffic on U.S. 191 except for an occasional eighteen-wheeler headed north.

On his left rose the majestic LaSal Mountains, now backlighted by the rising sun. A gold luminescence outlined the peaks, highlighting the shape of Moab's eastern horizon now so familiar to him. Wispy clouds of pink, crimson, and purple hung over the mountains, producing another world-class sunrise. Rivera considered the daily appearance of gaudy sunrises and sunsets as a special gift to those adventuresome souls who chose to live in the high desert. The profusion of light and color emerging from the darkness normally would have elevated his spirits.

But today was different. Rivera felt unsettled and dispirited after last night's conversation with Amy. She was beautiful, smart, and fun to be with—but she was also a strong-willed professional woman with firm plans for her career. For the first time since they had begun seeing each other, he sensed that their relationship might be in jeopardy.

All his life, he'd assumed he would meet someone wonderful, get married, have a family, and settle down in a place where he could spend the rest of his life. He thought he'd found the *place* when he moved to Moab. And he thought he'd found the *someone* when he met Amy. Then last night, all that had been turned upside down. He'd been aware of the impending problem all along, but he'd always managed to push it out of his consciousness back into a remote corner of his brain to be considered at a later date. Now, the time was fast approaching when he needed to deal with it. Amy made it clear last night that she'd go wherever necessary to advance her career, and change jobs and locations whenever a better opportunity presented itself.

He'd also learned during their conversation that she wasn't sure she wanted children. Her goals were to achieve a prominent position in the academic world of botany, become a tenured professor at a top-tier university, and hopefully someday be selected as a member of the National Academy of Sciences. Rivera knew she cared about him but it was clear her career would dominate her life's planning.

Something his grandfather had told him years ago popped into his head. *Marry someone whose values match your own.* His grandfather, from whom he'd often sought counsel, seemed to have a profound understanding of the trade-offs in life. He was a retired carpenter who had the wisdom of a philosopher and the mind of a renaissance man. Now his grandfather's words hung heavy in Rivera's heart. Could it be his and Amy's values were so different that they could never be resolved? He pondered that question as he drove, trying to confront it objectively, but encountering an emotional reluctance to give himself an honest answer.

He reached the town of Monticello and turned left on U.S. 491, heading toward the city of Cortez in the southwest corner of Colorado. He took a sip of coffee and thought about Albuquerque. It was a great city, not too large and not too small, sitting at the base of the Sandia Mountains. There were good restaurants, good people, a pleasant climate, and the internationally-famous annual Hot Air Balloon Fiesta. He'd visited there many times and had always enjoyed it. And it wasn't far from Four Corners, the geographic center of the high-desert canyon country he loved. An added advantage was that he'd be only three hours north of his family and friends in Las Cruces. Maybe he *should* leave Moab and move back to New Mexico.

Amy had made a good point when she said he hated working for Sheriff Campbell. Campbell was a retired street cop from Detroit who knew little about law enforcement in a rural area. He treated people as though he were still back in Detroit, hassling and arresting gang bangers. The contrast between Campbell and Leroy Bradshaw, his former boss, was extraordinary. They were polar opposites. Making the transition from Bradshaw-as-boss to Campbell-as-boss grated on Rivera's nerves and tried his patience on a daily basis.

There was also the possibility of a long-distance relationship with Amy—Rivera in Moab, she in Albuquerque, the two meeting somewhere in between on weekends. The more he considered that idea, the more it left him with a cold and empty feeling. He liked having Amy nearby and he suspected that most long-distance relationships eventually failed due to inattention. Besides, there wouldn't be much chance for family life that way.

Another possibility was the long-standing job offer he had from Leroy Bradshaw in Santa Fe. Bradshaw had done well since starting his private investigations firm. He'd assembled a competent staff and built a loyal base of A-list clients. Living in Santa Fe would put Rivera only about an hour from Albuquerque. He loved the idea of working for Bradshaw but had to admit he had a hard time picturing himself as a private detective.

Rivera shook his head. There were a lot of options and possibilities to consider, but this wasn't the time to do it—he needed to focus his thoughts on the Archuleta case. He drove past Sleeping Ute Mountain and headed south toward Shiprock, passing the *Welcome to New Mexico* sign and entering the Navajo nation.

He wondered what he would learn about Archuleta when he visited the village of Santa Elena and spoke to his family. More importantly, he wondered whether he had any real chance of identifying the young man's killer. Rivera had no preconceived notions about what he was looking for. He'd just have to question the people who knew Archuleta and feel his way forward—see where the facts took him.

He loved the challenge of investigative work. The beginning of each new case was like opening a box containing a giant jigsaw puzzle. Each piece represented a fact. The idea was to try to interconnect the facts in some sensible way until a larger picture emerged and became clear. Enough facts coupled with the right logic usually broke the case. The converse was also true—logic applied to too few facts would produce a distorted picture leading to incorrect conclusions. Rivera knew the biggest problem he would face in a fifteen-year-old case was extracting accurate information from a jumble of opinions, foggy memories, and biased points of view.

He turned east at Shiprock and continued on U.S. 64, soon leaving the Big Rez, as the locals called the Navajo Reservation—*Big* because it was the size of New England. He wondered what kind of reception awaited him at the Rio Arriba County Sheriff's Office. The interim sheriff seemed like a normal law enforcement guy but his deputy, Gilbert Jaramillo, sounded like he might be a problem. He told himself not to worry about it—just take things as they come.

Rivera passed a sign that said *Entering Rio Arriba County* and soon found himself driving across the Jicarilla Apache Nation. He'd been gaining altitude for the last hour and the foliage was becoming thicker and greener. Juniper and pinyon pines now dominated the landscape, replacing the rabbit brush, snakeweed, and sagebrush of the lower elevations. Soon he saw stands of pine trees. He glanced at his watch. It was a little after eleven o'clock. There was enough time for him to stop in Chama and get a bite to eat.

He ate a ham sandwich at a small diner and, before leaving town, stopped at the Cumbres and Toltec narrow gauge railroad terminal to pick up a brochure. He'd always wanted to take Amy on the 64-mile train ride to Antonito, Colorado. It seemed like a romantic trip that she would enjoy, if ever he could pull her away from her work. His brother had taken the trip with his wife for their tenth anniversary and told Rivera it was some of the most beautiful high valley and mountain country he'd ever seen.

Rivera left Chama and drove south to Tierra Amarilla, the small community which served as the county seat of Rio Arriba County. He parked in front of the old courthouse which was now boarded up, having been replaced by a modern building complex across the street. Rivera smiled, remembering his first trip through Tierra Amarilla many years ago. He'd needed a bathroom break and went into the courthouse looking for a men's room. In the basement he found a bathroom with the letter *M* on the door. He pushed it open and went inside. He looked around and found no urinals. Then a woman came out of one of the stalls, looked at him, gasped and covered her mouth in surprise, and retreated back into the stall. He excused himself and exited the bathroom, realizing then that the *M* stood for *Mujeres.* He went farther down the hall and found the bathroom with the letter *H* on the door, the place where all good *Hombres* went to relieve themselves. Sheriff Gallegos had said most people in the county spoke Spanish instead of English. He wasn't exaggerating.

After a brief search, Rivera found the sheriff's building a couple of blocks from the old courthouse. On a flagpole next to the building, a U.S. flag rippled in the breeze. Flying below it was a New Mexico state flag, a red Zia sun symbol on a field of yellow. He parked his pickup curbside and entered the building.

A slightly chubby, young receptionist named Ruby greeted him with a smile and a flirty manner. Her hair was long and her skirt was short. She asked Rivera to please have a seat in the reception area while she informed the sheriff of his arrival. The reception area, as it turned out, consisted of three straight back chairs pushed up against the front window. He sat down and surveyed the meager surroundings.

The building was minimal, about the size of a double-wide trailer. It was divided into rooms by temporary partitions. File boxes were stacked floor to ceiling along one wall. Across the room, Rivera spotted a deputy sitting at a corner desk, staring at him and sizing him up in an obviously disrespectful manner. He was overweight and sloppy looking, probably in his early fifties. He had brown hair and hooded brown eyes, and he was long overdue for a haircut. He slowly rose from his chair, hoisted up his belt, and sauntered over to where Rivera was seated. Stood over him.

He smiled, exposing a crooked set of yellowish teeth. "You the deputy from Utah?" He pronounced Utah like *Oo-tah.*

His nametag read *Jaramillo.* He was the rude deputy Rivera had spoken to on the phone. Rivera stood up. "That's right."

"Ain't you a little out of your jurisdiction, Amigo?"

"I'm here to visit the sheriff." Rivera felt his cheeks flush a little bit. He wasn't in the mood for games. He took a step toward the deputy and forced a smile. "That a problem for you, Amigo?"

Jaramillo took a step back, recovered awkwardly, and attempted a sinister expression. He was five eleven, same as Rivera, but he looked to be all beer gut and not much muscle. Rivera waited. If Jaramillo made a move toward him, Rivera wouldn't hesitate to deal with him—he disliked rude policemen.

A second man in uniform came hustling out of his office and quickly inserted himself between Rivera and Jaramillo. He was a stocky man about six feet tall with light brown eyes, thinning gray hair, and a walrus moustache. He looked to be about sixty and his nametag read *Gallegos.* He was the interim sheriff Rivera had spoken with on the phone.

Gallegos looked at Jaramillo with an expression somewhere between exasperation and disbelief. "I'll handle this, Gilbert."

Jaramillo remained in place.

The sheriff's voice went up a few decibels. "I said I'll handle this. Back to your desk, Gilbert."

Jaramillo gave Rivera one last cold stare and then walked back to his desk.

Gallegos extended his hand. "I'm Ruben Gallegos. Let's go into my office and talk." He turned to the receptionist. "Ruby, bring us some coffee, please."

The office, a cubicle constructed of six-foot high transparent partitions, was small and minimally furnished. The sheriff's desk was gray metal, just like Rivera's back in Moab. A couple of visitor's chairs sat in front of the desk and an empty table sat against the wall. A single window looked out at a vine-covered wooden fence. Cardboard boxes were stacked in one corner of the room and the air smelled of cigarette smoke. Rivera sat down in one of the chairs.

Ruby returned with a small Styrofoam cup in each hand and presented one to each man. Before leaving, she turned to Rivera, curtsied, and smiled a flirty smile. "Will there be anything else, Deputy Rivera?"

"That'll be all, Ruby," said the sheriff. "Thank you."

Ruby lingered a long moment, gazing at Rivera, then sashayed out of the office.

"Watch out for Ruby," said the sheriff with a wry grin. "She's looking for a husband."

After some preliminaries about Moab and the drive to Tierra Amarilla, Gallegos closed the office door. "Jaramillo loves to eavesdrop. He can still hear over the partitions but this'll make it a little harder for him."

Rivera smiled and nodded. So far, everything about Rio Arriba County seemed strange and different.

"These are temporary quarters for us while the new sheriff's office is being constructed," said Gallegos. "The new digs are a lot better than this place. I'm sheriff only on an interim basis as I told you on the phone. I'm a retired senior deputy. They called me out of retirement after our former sheriff was sent to prison about seven months ago. He was allowed to serve as sheriff the whole time he was on trial. It was an awkward time. I got disgusted working in that environment and retired about halfway through the trial. I'm here because the county commissioners asked me to come back and serve as sheriff until the next election and because, frankly, I could use some extra money. My wife and I had big plans for retirement—winters in Baja California and all that. Then her diabetes took a turn for the worse and the medical bills started piling up."

Gallegos took a sip of coffee and paused, as if organizing his thoughts. He nodded toward Jaramillo who was now sitting at his desk and talking on the phone.

"Gilbert Jaramillo thought he should have gotten the job as sheriff but everyone knows he's, shall we say, marginally competent. He's been sulking ever since I took over. I don't mean to be unkind, but basically, all he's good for is running errands. I can't fire him because, being just an interim sheriff, I don't really have much authority. And more importantly, Gilbert is the nephew of Señor Fernando Dominguez. Don Fernando is considered the patriarch of Rio Arriba County. He is the descendant of Don Carlo Dominguez and the sole living heir to Don Carlo's Mexican land grant, over 18,000 acres of the best land in this part of the county. Don Fernando is highly respected and revered by the people, and he's very generous to those in the community needing assistance. He has everyone's loyalty. And he is the final authority in resolving disputes throughout Rio Arriba County. He is definitely not someone to be trifled with. Therefore, I must put up with his nephew."

Rivera nodded as though that made sense to him, but it made no sense at all. Since when did counties have patriarchs? And who in the United States uses the title *Don* anymore? So far, Rio Arriba County seemed like it was right out of an old black-and-white movie set in Mexico. "This is very different from what I'm used to," Rivera managed.

"That's why I'm telling you all this. You need to understand how things work in Rio Arriba County before you go poking around, especially in the small villages." He leaned forward, raised his eyebrows, and lowered his voice. "If you get into trouble, there's a limit as to how much I can help you."

Rivera nodded. "I understand." He didn't really, but didn't know what else to say.

"You said that after you inform Archuleta's family about his death, you want to begin an investigation here."

"That's correct. Now that we have our victim's identity, we can finally move forward with an investigation."

"He was killed fifteen years ago. Do you really expect to find his killer now?"

"I'm going to try."

"Well, if I can help with that, let me know. But understand this—unless there's clear evidence linking his death to someone in my jurisdiction, I'm not getting involved. There's no way I'm going to stir up the citizens of Rio Arriba County if it's just a witch hunt. These people have been through some tough times in their history. Most of them are good and decent folks but they've been screwed over by outsiders for centuries. So they don't trust lawmen or anyone else associated with the government—and I mean all levels of government. They harbor a deep resentment toward authority. If you irritate them enough, they're apt to rise up and start a revolt. It's happened here before. That's not something I want to see while I'm in this office."

"I'll tread as lightly as I can." Rivera wasn't sure what the sheriff meant about the people being screwed over by outsiders, but it was something he intended to learn more about.

"I've asked Deputy Sheriff Gloria Valdez to accompany you to Santa Elena so you can inform the Archuleta family about their son. I'd go with you myself but I'm tied up with the District Attorney this afternoon." He looked at his watch. "In fact, I've got to head over to his office right now. Gloria will meet you here in about an hour. Meanwhile, unless you have some questions, I'd suggest you drive around Tierra Amarilla and get acquainted with the area."

Rivera thanked the sheriff and took his advice. He hopped into his pickup and began exploring the small community. The central part of town, to Rivera's eyes, was not particularly attractive. Across the street from the sheriff's office was a decrepit, tan, one story building that looked like it had been abandoned for decades. The doors and windows were boarded up. Faded lettering painted above the door proclaimed the building had once been Lito's Ballroom.

He drove slowly down each street to get oriented to his new surroundings. Although closed now, the old courthouse was still the centerpiece of town. A few small enterprises located in the immediate area were open for business. Others were vacant. Several older buildings in the town center were abandoned and disintegrating with age. A block away, he came upon the *Santo Niño* Catholic Church, a small building with tan stucco walls and a metal roof. In front of the church was a stone grotto with a statue of the Blessed Virgin in flowing light blue and white robes.

From there, he toured several residential streets. The houses were modest and widely separated from one another. Most were constructed of adobe bricks, rock, or concrete blocks. Pickup trucks seemed to be the vehicle of choice.

He left the town center and drove a few blocks back to the main highway. Tierra Amarilla was situated on rolling hills at the intersection of U.S. 84 and U.S. 64. A gas station, grocery store, and a few other small businesses were located on U.S. 84, the north-south highway. The layout of the town seemed random, as though it had evolved without much of a plan. Rivera had gotten used to the cities and towns of Utah where the Mormons had laid out each settlement with a well thought out matrix of streets. Roadways there were wide and straight, and the street nomenclature was consistent from one town to the next.

He was puzzled by a large billboard prominently displayed at the south end of town. It read, *Tierra o Muerte, ¡Zapata vive!* Land or Death, long live Zapata! A likeness of the face of Emiliano Zapata, the famous Mexican rebel, was pictured on the billboard. His dark, soulful eyes stared at anyone driving north on U.S. 84 into Tierra Amarilla.

To Rivera, Tierra Amarilla was not the type of town that reached out and embraced you with warm, welcoming arms. It seemed foreign to him in so many ways.

7

AFTER CRUISING THE streets of Tierra Amarilla in his Grand County Sheriff's Department vehicle for an hour, and receiving curious stares from the locals, Rivera returned to the sheriff's office. A smiling Deputy Sheriff Gloria Valdez was waiting at the front door to greet him. She had a striking oval face, mysterious and attractive, with pale green eyes. She was about five-feet-six inches tall and her dark hair was gathered in a ponytail. Her light brown skin was perfect except for a tiny scar on the left side of her chin. She looked to be in her early thirties. She introduced herself and gave Rivera a firm handshake.

"Let's go sit in the conference room and talk," she said.

Like the sheriff's office, the conference room was made up of six-foot high transparent partitions. It contained a long wooden table and six gray metal chairs. As they sat down, Rivera noticed Gloria wasn't wearing a wedding ring.

She took a long look at Rivera's face and smiled. "Sheriff Gallegos asked me to escort you to Santa Elena."

"I appreciate it very much."

After some get-acquainted talk, Gloria asked him about the Archuleta case. He explained it to her in detail, starting with the call he'd received from Mrs. Foster and the promise he'd made to her. He briefed her on the items he'd found in the barn and ran through the limited information in the case file. As he spoke, he noticed that Gilbert Jaramillo had repositioned himself at an empty desk closer to the conference room. Rivera guessed he'd moved there to eavesdrop on their conversation. He saw that Gloria had also noticed him, but she didn't seem to mind the intrusion into their privacy.

"So I'm here for two reasons," said Rivera. "First, I need to notify Archuleta's family about his death. Then I want to see what I can learn about his life and who might have had a reason to kill him. It's an old case, but I'm hoping I can uncover some useful information by interviewing his family and neighbors."

Gloria smiled and produced a doubtful expression. "You'll probably find the people up there reluctant to talk to you—they're not used to outsiders. Like most of the small villages in the mountains, Santa Elena is an unusual place. I've visited there a few times for various reasons, mostly calls about a *bruja* named Josefina who lives in a small cabin nearby. Sometimes she goes into the village and stirs up trouble. People in those small communities take witches seriously. If a *bruja* gives someone the *mal ojo,* we usually get called about it. There's not much you can do except try to calm everyone down. The bad eye from a witch, they believe, causes some serious bad luck. So anything unfortunate that happens to a person after he or she receives a *mal ojo* is attributed to the *mal ojo,* whether or not there was any real connection. When you're raised from childhood with those beliefs, it's hard to ignore them later in life even though they may not be logical." She thought for a long moment. "You're going to find Santa Elena is very different from what you are used to."

Rivera studied her. "Do you believe in witchcraft?"

"Let's just say I have a healthy respect for the effect it can have on people who believe in its powers."

"But you don't believe in it yourself?"

There was a long pause. "I didn't say that."

Rivera nodded. Decided to change the subject. "Do you know the Archuletas?"

"Archuleta is a fairly common name in northern New Mexico and southern Colorado. I know some of them but I've never met the Santa Elena Archuletas."

"What else can you tell me about Santa Elena? I understand there are only about 300 people living there."

"The village is what's left of an old Mexican land grant. It used to be much larger, but the U. S.

government took away all the communal lands that were part of the land grant. Only the individual tracts—a small fraction of the original land grant—remain in private hands."

"I remember learning a little about land grants in school but I don't know as much as I should. I know they're large parcels of land that were awarded to frontier people by the government of Spain and later Mexico. As I recall, the grants are sort of like the land the U.S. government parceled out to homesteaders willing to help settle the west. But what's the distinction between communal and private lands?"

"It's kind of a long story."

"I'm interested. I'd like to hear it."

"Well, it all started sometime after Spain invaded Mexico in the 1500s and subjugated the indigenous peoples. The Spanish government began awarding land grants to select Spaniards in order to help settle the land and establish permanent communities. The grants were quite large—from a few thousand acres to a few hundred thousand. Back then, Mexico was huge. It included what are now the states of California, Arizona, New Mexico, Texas, and parts of Nevada, Utah, and Colorado. After Mexico drove out the Spaniards in 1821, the Mexican government continued the practice of awarding land grants. The grants were given either on an individual or communal basis. If the land grant was awarded to an individual, it was considered all private land. In most cases, though, the grant was made to a group of individuals and was therefore communal."

"Why were most of the land grants communal?"

"Because groups fared better on the frontier than individuals. It took many people to clear land, dig acequias to irrigate the fields, build homes, and defend themselves against the Indians. Communal grants were set up with small individual tracts, one for each family where they could build a house, and a very large communal tract to be used by everyone in the group for hunting, grazing, and cutting timber for buildings and firewood."

"I see. So why did the federal government take the communal property?"

"This is where it gets interesting. And heartbreaking. When James K. Polk became president in 1845, he had one large goal in mind—to push the western boundary of the United States all the way to the Pacific Ocean. You probably know this part—he invaded Mexico on a questionable pretext and conquered it against little resistance. The Treaty of Guadalupe Hidalgo was signed by the two countries in 1848 to end the hostilities. To settle the matter, the United States took the northern half of Mexico and in return paid the Mexican government fifteen million dollars. And now we come to the important part of the story. In the treaty, the U.S. government agreed to honor all Spanish and Mexican land grants. Then, after the fact, instead of honoring them as agreed to, the U.S. government decided to establish a commission empowered to review each land grant and decide whether it was valid. That's when the games began and the real trouble started."

Rivera watched Gloria's eyes as she spoke. He'd never seen pale green eyes like hers before. Like deep pools of water. "What kind of games?"

"The commission decided that the individual land grants fell under the Treaty of Guadalupe Hidalgo and were therefore honored. The communal land grants were treated differently. For those, only the portion made up of individual tracts was honored. The communal portion, the vast majority of the land, was not. Communal land grants were a common arrangement under Spanish Law but there was no equivalent in English law, so the Federal Government took ownership of all the communal lands. The owners of the individual tracts could hardly support themselves without the communal lands, so many of them eventually moved away."

"That doesn't seem fair."

"It wasn't. At first, the federal land grab made little difference. People continued using the common lands just as they did before the government took possession of them. There was no one there to stop them. But that soon changed. The government started making rules about what could and couldn't be done on what was previously communal land, and employed people to enforce the rules. That's when the trouble started. And it's still going on today."

"You seem to know quite a lot about land grants."

She produced a bitter expression. "I should. I'm a descendant of Juan Bautista Valdez who received a Spanish land grant in 1807. The grant was for 147,500 acres around Cañones. When the U.S. government got through taking what wasn't theirs, all that was left to the Valdez descendants was 1,468 acres."

"Is that what happened in Santa Elena?"

"Yeah, it was pretty much the same thing. Santa Elena was originally a Mexican land grant of 47,400 acres. Then, after the treaty, the U.S. government took the communal lands—they now exist as part of Carson National Forest. Only 3,200 acres of the original grant remain in private hands. As a result, the people who live in Santa Elena feel a strong resentment toward the government. In some cases, it's a quiet hatred that will probably erupt some day in violence. I tell you all this because it will probably affect the way you are received in Santa Elena."

Rivera nodded. "What else can you tell me about the village?"

"It's small tight-knit community in the foothills of the Tusas Mountains. It's located about ten miles northeast of Canjilon. If you don't know how to get there, it's a little hard to find. There's some farming there and a little ranching. Some of the ranching is carried out secretly on nearby national forest lands, illegally of course. People don't want to pay for grazing permits on land they feel was stolen from their ancestors. It's a long story, but the people have a legitimate beef. Want to drive out there now and see it?"

"Sure. Should I follow you in my unit?"

"That's probably not a good idea. A Utah police vehicle suddenly appearing in Santa Elena might alarm the people." She smiled. "You might end up on the receiving end of a *mal ojo*. Let's go in my unit. The people are used to seeing Rio Arriba Sheriff's Office vehicles."

As they headed for the door, Rivera noticed Deputy Jaramillo had returned to his desk and was now intently dialing his telephone. Rivera got the impression he was calling someone to report the details of Rivera's conversation with Gloria.

Gloria pulled out of the parking lot and drove slowly through town. "First time in Rio Arriba County?"

"I visited the Ghost Ranch once and Abiquiu once and I've driven through Tierra Amarilla several times."

"The locals call it T.A. for short." She smiled. "What do you think of it so far?"

"It's different."

Her smile erupted into laughter. "I've heard that."

Rivera couldn't get Jaramillo off his mind. "I think your Deputy Gilbert Jaramillo would rather I not be here."

"Don't mind him. He treats most strangers that way." She didn't elaborate.

They drove south out of Tierra Amarilla, past the billboard that had attracted Rivera's attention.

"What can you tell me about that billboard?"

"I don't know who put it up but it's been there for as long as I can remember. It represents a simmering resentment of the heavy-handed actions of the U.S. government. In the beginning, this land was occupied only by native people. There were no boundaries—the Indians didn't map hard lines of ownership onto the landscape. Then the Europeans showed up and began parceling out land grants. Boundaries and barbed-wire fences began to appear. You know what happened after that—most of the land was appropriated by the U.S. government. Emiliano Zapata's image is on the billboard because he was an iconic figure in the Mexican Revolution in the early 1900s. He fought the Mexican government for land reform on behalf of the indigenous peasants of Chiapas. His followers were known as Zapatistas. He's kind of a folk hero to the people around here. Some of the locals think of themselves as modern-day Zapatistas." She paused. "A lot of these folks hope that one day the land that was taken from their ancestors will be returned, or at least they'll be compensated in some way for their loss."

"Do you think that will ever happen?"

She thought for a long moment. "I hope so, but probably not."

About 15 miles south of Tierra Amarilla, Gloria made a left turn off the highway onto a two-lane asphalt road that led to Canjilon. The road steadily rose as it entered forest land densely populated with ponderosa pine trees. Just when it seemed the road would take them higher and higher into the mountains, it crested a hill and began descending into a scenic treeless valley cut by a small stream. Nestled in the center of the valley was the settlement of Canjilon. From the highway, Rivera would never have guessed there was a community hidden behind the pines. He unfolded a map he'd brought along.

"Interesting looking village. What's the population of Canjilon?"

"Around three hundred, about the same as Santa Elena. The county has many small villages like this."

They crossed a bridge over a small creek and turned left on a narrow road which was marked Route 559 on Rivera's map.

"This road winds through the Tusas Range for about 30 miles and eventually comes out on the east side of the mountains at a small town called El Rito. The road is passable most of the time but can be a big problem in winter. El Rito is another small village, one of the oldest in the county."

Rivera couldn't get the land grant business out of his mind. "When I was studying Rio Arriba County on the internet, I read that there was an attack on your courthouse back in the 1960s that was related to land grants."

She smiled. "That's right. A man named Reies Tijerina organized the descendants of pioneers whose land grant property had been taken by the U.S. government. They intended to take back their land, by force if necessary. They were some of our Zapatistas. One day in 1967, Tijerina and a band of armed revolutionaries invaded the Rio Arriba County courthouse. Their plan was to make a citizen's arrest of the district attorney who had earlier ordered the arrest of some of Tijerina's followers. There was a big shootout wounding a couple of men on each side. The FBI got involved and the revolutionaries escaped into the mountains." She chuckled. "Weeks later, there were actually military tanks driving the mountain roads looking for these guys. Some of the citizens around here were so angry with the Feds, they wanted to secede from the union. Never underestimate the resentment of Rio Arriba citizens to government authority."

They continued on the narrow road, higher and higher through the shade of the pine trees until they came to a gravel road leading off to the left. They turned, now headed north, gaining altitude as they drove through the forest. They splashed across a small creek and came to an open meadow where a herd of mule deer was grazing. As the vehicle approached them, the deer raised their heads and stared at the steel intruder, muscles tightened. One skittish deer retreated a few steps which, an instant later, triggered a thundering exodus as the herd sprinted for the trees.

A half mile farther up the road, they came to another clearing. On the left side of the road, Rivera saw a massive stone entrance to a ranch. An asphalt driveway led across the clearing and into the trees on the far side. He thought it incongruous that a private asphalt driveway would connect to a gravel county road. A wrought iron sign arched over the entryway displaying the name *Dominguez* in bronze letters.

"What's that?" asked Rivera.

"That's the estate of Don Fernando Dominguez. He's one of the lucky ones. He is a descendant of Don Carlo Dominguez who received a Mexican land grant for 18,200 acres. It was an individual grant with no communal property so the U.S. Government approved the entire grant. He has eleven children, and many of them still live on the estate. His wife passed away a couple of years ago."

Rivera nodded, remembering. "He's the one the sheriff was telling me about. He referred to him as the patriarch of the county."

"Right. He's one of the most revered men in this part of New Mexico. He's the one the villagers around here go to for help in resolving their disputes. He's an exceptionally fine gentleman, in the tradition of a true Spanish *hidalgo*."

"A nobleman. You don't hear that word used much anymore."

"He's not only a nobleman, he's also very lucky. A molybdenum deposit was discovered on the back end of his property about thirty years ago. It's now an operating mine and Don Fernando has become one of the wealthiest men in New Mexico."

"Impressive. I'd like to drive in there and see it someday."

"I would too, but I think it's by invitation only." She laughed. "And I've never been invited."

"Eleven kids. That's a huge family."

"And some of them are quite accomplished. His daughter Maria is a mezzo-soprano and has performed at the Metropolitan Opera. His son Julio runs the moly mine and is also one of the three Rio Arriba county commissioners. His son Alberto, who could have doubled for Clark Gable, is a state senator. I hear he's being groomed for lieutenant governor. And his son Rafael is supposed to be a financial wizard. He owns some kind of big investment company in Santa Fe. The rest of Don Fernando's children live on the estate."

"He must be very proud of his family." As soon as he uttered the word *family*, Rivera's thoughts reverted to Amy. He began replaying in his mind their conversation at La Jacaranda and started wondering again about their future. Would they find a way to stay together or would he have to start looking for someone all over again? Maybe staying in Moab wasn't worth losing her.

Gloria interrupted his thoughts. "At the other end of the spectrum is Josefina, the *bruja* I told you about. She lives on the estate too, in a modest cabin in the woods. No one knows why Don Fernando is so kind to her. There are a lot of theories. Some say he's generous with her so she won't send bad luck his way. Others say he uses her to cast spells on his competitors. And some say he doesn't believe in witchcraft at all but knows Josefina is an old woman of modest means who needs food and a place to live. Take your pick."

A tall, handsome man dressed in black was sitting on a dark brown horse near the front gate. He had a thin, dark moustache and looked to be in his early fifties. He reminded Rivera of a character from an old Spanish movie. The horse was a breed Rivera didn't recognize but it was a magnificent specimen. The man smiled at Gloria and touched the brim of his Spanish-style hat as they passed.

"That's Eduardo Salazar. He's the chief of security for Don Fernando's estate and lives there with his family. I met him during the trial of the previous sheriff. He was in the courtroom as a spectator every day. I'm sure he was there to report the courtroom proceedings back to Don Fernando. The Don was a supporter of the former sheriff. He believed in him and had thrown his weight behind him each time the former sheriff ran for re-election. The man served as sheriff for twenty years before going to prison last year. I heard Don Fernando was embarrassed and angry when he learned the person he'd handpicked for sheriff turned out to be a crook."

They crested another hill and began descending from the forest into another tree-less valley. A small village was nestled in the heart of the valley.

"That's Santa Elena," said Gloria.

8

FROM A DISTANCE, Santa Elena looked like what Rivera had seen on Google Earth—a residential community about four blocks long and two blocks wide nestled in a high valley in the middle of the forest. Outside the village proper were cultivated green fields and grazing land surrounded by barbed wire fences. The village lay still and peaceful looking, plumes of white smoke rising from the chimneys.

"Pretty village," said Rivera. "What are the people like?"

"Most of these small mountain villages are populated with good, hard working, independent people. For the most part, they keep to themselves. They have little interest in what's happening in the outside world."

"Where do they work?"

"Some have jobs in T.A., some work in Española. But many are tradesman and work right here in the village. The rest are farmers and midnight ranchers."

"Midnight ranchers?"

"They're the ones who secretly graze their cattle on government land."

"What about the kids. Where do they go to school?"

"The school bus picks them up and takes them to T.A. Most of the women stay at home, cooking and sewing and keeping house. Some of them bake goods for sale."

"Like old times."

"Exactly."

As they drove down the main street of Santa Elena, Rivera could see that most of the homes were constructed of adobe bricks sealed with stucco cement. Nearly all had metal roofs and rock chimneys. Many of the doors and window frames were painted turquoise. Old pickup trucks were parked here and there. The main road through the village was asphalt which had been patched and re-patched, and the side roads were gravel. A community water well had been drilled near the center of the village. A few of the dwellings were abandoned and in a state of disrepair, their thick adobe walls dissolving and sagging wherever the stucco protection had cracked and fallen off. Lawns here were nonexistent—most of the yards were dirt.

Rivera pointed to one of the homes. "Turquoise seems to be a popular color here," he said.

"It's the color that wards off evil spirits," said Gloria.

Rivera looked at her face. She was serious.

Midway through town, they passed a small church constructed of freshly painted white clapboard. A steeple with a small brass bell rose from the roof. In front of the church was a stone grotto with a statue Rivera recognized as the Virgin of Guadalupe. A white, wooden fence surrounded the church yard.

Except for a young boy riding a small bicycle with training wheels, the town appeared empty. The boy stopped and stared when he saw the vehicle approaching. He was wearing a striped T-shirt, jeans with holes in the knees, and sneakers. Gloria brought the vehicle to a halt, rolled down the window, smiled, and spoke to him in Spanish.

"Hello there. How old are you?"

The boy held up six fingers.

"I used to have a bicycle just like that."

The boy stood there in silence, staring at her with large, brown eyes.

"We have come to visit the Archuleta family. Can you tell us which house they live in?"

He hesitated, then shook his head.

"Do you know if they live here in Santa Elena?"

Now the boy appeared confused and frightened. He abandoned his bicycle and ran down the street to the front door of one of the houses. He looked back once, then opened the door, entered, and closed the door behind him.

"He's probably never seen a lady cop before," said Gloria. "Or any cop."

"Or maybe he's been told not to give information to strangers," said Rivera.

Gloria drove to the house the boy had entered while Rivera retrieved the bike and followed along behind the vehicle. He noticed in some of the houses he passed that pairs of eyes were watching him through the windows. He pushed the bike into the boy's yard.

Gloria knocked on the door through which the boy had disappeared, and, after a long delay, a woman opened it a few inches and peered out at them. Gloria apologized for the intrusion and for frightening the boy, then asked where the Archuletas lived. The woman's eyes shifted back and forth between Gloria and Rivera, as though trying to decide what to do. Then her small, brown, calloused hand came through the opening. She silently pointed to the house across the street and closed the door.

The two deputies crossed the street to the Archuleta residence, another small home constructed with adobe bricks and a slathered-on stucco coating. A 1970s-vintage Chevy pickup truck was parked in front, its bed filled with cut logs and a chainsaw. Five calico kittens were playing in the front yard while the mother cat sat on a weathered, wooden chair and watched.

Rivera wasn't looking forward to meeting Archuleta's family. Several times during his career as a deputy, the task of informing parents that their child was dead had fallen upon him. Usually it was a rock climbing accident or an overturned kayak in the rapids, but occasionally it was murder. Leroy Bradshaw had counseled him not to hesitate in delivering the bad news. *Just tell them straight out. Beating around the bush won't change the facts or make the bad news any easier to swallow.*

Rivera removed his hat. He took a deep breath, let it out, and knocked on the door. A woman about sixty years old pulled the door part way open and looked out at him. She was tall and slim, with long dark hair pinned to the top of her head. She looked like an older version of the woman he'd seen in the photograph in Archuleta's wallet. She appeared wary as Rivera introduced himself and Gloria. He spoke in Spanish.

"May we come in? I have some news."

She opened the door and without a word, gestured them toward a couple of stuffed chairs in the living room. She sat opposite them on a couch with a floral design. The house was warm, spotless, and furnished with old but tasteful pieces. A vase of fresh spring flowers sat on an end table and a fire was crackling in the fireplace. On the wall was a framed photograph of a young man whose face looked just like the one on David Archuleta's driver's license. There was an array of tin crucifixes surrounding the photo. Below it, on a small table, were three carved *santo* figures and a half-dozen votive candles.

Mrs. Archuleta's eyes were beginning to well up with tears. She had a look of fear on her face, as though she knew what Rivera was about to tell her.

"Fifteen years ago, a young man was found dead in the LaSal Mountains near Moab, Utah. It wasn't until yesterday that we were able to identify him."

The woman's shoulders sagged. Her lower lip quivered and tears began running down her cheeks. "That was my David, wasn't it?"

He nodded. "Yes, I'm afraid so."

"I knew it as soon as I opened the door and saw you standing there." She buried her face in her hands, shuddered, and wept. "I guess I knew he was dead," she said, speaking through her tears. "If he was alive, he'd have stayed in touch with his mother. I always hoped he would come home one day—just show up, put his arms around me and say, 'Mama, I'm home.'"

Gloria rose from her chair, sat next to the woman, and put her arm around her. Mrs. Archuleta rubbed her eyes with her fingertips. "Well, at least now we know for sure. How did my David die?"

"He was shot in the chest. He died instantly so I doubt he felt any pain." Rivera wasn't sure about the pain part, but he wanted to soften the blow any way he could.

Mrs. Archuleta looked surprised. "He was shot? With a gun?"

Rivera nodded. "Yes. A rifle. We have reason to believe it was deliberate."

She grimaced. "Oh, *Dios mio,* he was always such a good boy. Who would do such a thing?"

"That's what I intend to find out. I know this is a bad time for you, but it would help me find David's killer if you could answer a few questions. Are you feeling up to it?"

She pulled a tissue from her pocket, blotted her nose, and nodded. "Yes, I think so."

Rivera took out his pen and notepad and began asking questions. First he covered the basics: family, friends, schooling, jobs, activities, interests. David Archuleta had two married sisters living in Española and a married brother living in Tierra Amarilla. His father had a job as an equipment operator working for the New Mexico Department of Transportation. David had been a good son, well-liked by everyone in the community. His mother described him as a poet and a lover of nature. She said he was very generous to those in the community needing help. He was active in the church and helped with the collection basket on Sunday. He also tended the church yard and helped with building maintenance. For money, he worked odd jobs in Santa Elena and sometimes worked with his father as a temporary employee at the highway department. He had two close friends with whom he'd grown up and attended school: Juan Baeza and Victor

Sanchez. Juan was deceased, and Victor had moved away many years ago.

"Did you report David's disappearance to the authorities?"

"Yes, I told the sheriff the day after David didn't come home. He said he would keep his eyes open but I never heard anything back from him. My husband asked at the sheriff's office many times but the sheriff always said they knew nothing. He promised to let us know if they learned anything. That sheriff turned out to be no good so I don't think he worked very hard trying to find my David."

"When your son was found, he had vertical lash marks on his back. Like he'd been whipped. Any idea how he'd gotten them?"

"My son was a Penitente, a member of the *cofradía* here in Santa Elena. He got those marks from lashing himself with his yucca fiber rope. You know, for penance." She spoke matter-of-factly as though that were normal and commonplace in all of society.

Rivera was vaguely familiar with the Penitentes. He'd learned about them in a Southwest history course he'd taken in college. Now he wished he'd paid more attention. They were some kind of Catholic lay religious group that held secret meetings in buildings called *moradas*. He was familiar with the Spanish word *cofradía*. It meant brotherhood or confraternity.

Beyond that, he could remember little, but he was curious to learn more.

"May I ask why he became a Penitente?

She seemed surprised at the question—as though Rivera should know better. "Because it was a great honor. He was invited to become a member at a young age. He was only nineteen but he was highly respected in the community. Not everyone is invited, you know."

"Did your son own a vehicle?" Rivera was still puzzled about how Archuleta had gotten to Moab.

"No. His friend Victor had a pickup truck. All three boys used it."

"Did your son have any enemies that you know of?"

"Oh, no. Everyone loved David."

Not everyone, Rivera thought to himself. "Do the families of Juan Baeza and Victor Sanchez still live in Santa Elena?

"Yes, they do." Mrs. Archuleta explained how to find their homes.

Rivera thanked her and got up to leave. "If there's anything I can do, any questions I can answer, please let me know."

"I do have one question, Deputy," said Mrs. Archuleta. "Where is my David now and how can I get him home? He should be buried here in Santa Elena so he can be with his family."

Rivera didn't know the answer to that question. "I'll find out where David is buried and help you get him home."

Rivera and Gloria followed Mrs. Archuleta's directions and found the Sanchez home. Rivera knocked on the front door and waited. He knocked again. There was no answer.

An old man, probably in his eighties, was hoeing a vegetable garden on the side of the house next door. Rivera approached him and asked if he knew when Mr. or Mrs. Sanchez might return home. The man looked up from his work, inspected Rivera through eyes clouded by cataracts, and shrugged. He returned to his work, using the corner of the hoe blade to deftly extract small weeds encroaching on his tomato plants.

"It's very important," said Rivera.

The old man looked up, produced another shrug. "Who knows? Maybe tomorrow."

Rivera and Gloria walked down the main street of the village toward the Baeza home which was a half block away.

"You were right," he said. "People here don't want to open up to strangers."

"They don't know us. They're fine people but they don't trust outsiders."

They knocked on the turquoise door of the Baeza home. Mrs. Baeza was a chunky, elderly woman with white hair and smooth, brown skin. She was wearing a white blouse and jeans. A light blue shawl was wrapped around her neck. After Rivera explained the nature of his visit, she invited them inside with obvious reluctance.

Mrs. Baeza was shocked to learn about David Archuleta. She looked pained and made a small cross on her forehead and her lips with her thumb. "Ay Dios mio! I am shocked to hear that. David was such a good boy. I thought he just left town, like the other one."

"Which other one?"

"Victor Sanchez. After David Archuleta disappeared and my Juan was killed, Victor disappeared too. The three of them were best friends."

"Wait a minute, Mrs. Baeza. Mrs. Archuleta told me your son had died but I didn't realize he'd been killed."

"He was shot in the woods about three miles from here. The sheriff said it was a hunting accident but I think he was killed deliberately." She shook her head, then shrugged. "Maybe the sheriff was right, I don't know, but that's what I think. People around here are good hunters. No one would mistake a human being for an animal. All the time around here, people shoot elk and deer and rabbits for food. The hunters don't shoot people."

Rivera was jotting notes into his notepad as fast as he could. "Let me be clear on the sequence of events. Was Juan shot before or after David disappeared?"

"Well let me see. First, David Archuleta disappeared. About two or three days later, my Juan was shot. Then, a few days after that, Victor Sanchez left town."

"Has anyone heard from Victor since he left?"

She shrugged. "No. Not as far as I know."

"What else can you tell me about your son?"

"He was a good boy. He played football in high school. He was handsome and the cheerleaders all made a fuss over him. No one in our family ever went to college and I'd always hoped Juan would be the first, but his grades weren't good enough. He spent too much time with those birds of his. He loved birds and was very proud of his collection. He kept them in those cages out back. He was always talking to them and bringing them things they liked to eat instead of doing his homework."

Rivera had always been interested in birds. Whenever he spent time in the backcountry, he was on the lookout for unusual species. "Birds? What kind of birds?"

She smiled. "All kinds."

"Where did he get the birds?"

She put her hand over her mouth as if she'd said something she shouldn't have. Then she shrugged. "I guess it doesn't matter now. Juan is gone. He told me to keep his bird collection secret, like he was doing something wrong by collecting them. I don't know exactly where he got them. Somewhere out in the forest, I guess."

"Don't worry. It's not a problem." Rivera didn't want to trouble her by telling her it was illegal to trap and possess certain birds. He was vague about the law himself, unclear on which birds were protected and which weren't. Besides, Mrs. Baeza was right—it didn't matter now. But Rivera was curious—he'd never come across a bird collector before. "Could I take a look at those cages?"

"Sure, but they're empty now." She led the deputies out the back door. Pointed.

Dozens of bird cages of all sizes were stacked against a rock wall in the rear. Some were large, about four feet on a side. Others were small, about the size of parakeet cages. All appeared to be homemade from wood and wire mesh.

"I let all the birds go free after Juan was killed," said Mrs. Baeza. "One of them, a red-tailed hawk I think, slashed my arm as I let him out of his cage." She showed Rivera a long scar on her forearm. "Ungrateful so-and-so."

Rivera walked over for a closer inspection. The cages were well constructed with fixed and swinging perches, water cups, and bottom trays for waste removal. Now there was nothing left in them except a few residual feathers. As he studied the workmanship, his eyes fell on some feathers at the bottom of one of the larger cages. Something about them looked familiar—something he'd seen recently. Then he remembered. They looked just like the feathers he'd seen in the workbench drawer in Foster's barn.

He pulled his iPhone from his pocket and stepped through the photos he'd taken there. He studied the photo of the empty drawer, the one with the dead bugs, spider webs, and feathers—the stuff he'd assumed was not originally in the backpack, just the detritus of a dirty barn. With his thumb and forefinger, he expanded the portion of the image that contained the feathers. Curious, he thought. They looked exactly like the feathers in Juan's cages.

Had Rivera been mistaken? Had the feathers in Foster's workbench actually come from Archuleta's backpack? Probably so, he figured, but what did that imply? Was it important to his case? He could think of no immediate answer.

He photographed the cages and their contents, not sure if the matching feathers had any significance. But Sheriff Leroy Bradshaw had taught him not to believe in coincidences. "*A coincidence usually means you're on the right track*," his old boss liked to say.

9

"KIND OF AN INTERESTING sequence of events, isn't it?" said Rivera. "Three close friends who grew up together in the same village. First, David Archuleta is murdered in the LaSal Mountains, then Juan Baeza is shot and killed down here, then Victor Sanchez leaves town, never to be seen again. All in the period of a week."

Gloria's green eyes were locked on the road as she drove through the mountains back to the Rio Arriba County sheriff's building. The sun was dropping in the west, creating long, mottled shadows across the road.

"That's a lot of coincidences," she said. "It's hard to believe there's not some kind of connection."

"I wonder what happened to Victor Sanchez. I hope we don't discover he was killed too."

"If he was still alive, you'd think he would've contacted someone in Santa Elena by now—or at least stayed in touch with his family. Mrs. Baeza made it sound like he just disappeared completely."

"There's one more coincidence." He told her about the feathers.

She shot him an incredulous glance. "You think those feathers might be important?"

Rivera laughed. "I'm not sure but I was trained by a man with a suspicious mind."

They passed Canjilon and headed toward U.S. 84.

"Any idea why David Archuleta's name was never entered into the National Crime Information Center's database as a missing person?" asked Rivera.

"Well, I've only been a deputy in the department for a couple of years so all that predates me. My guess is our former sheriff, the one who's thankfully now in prison, didn't feel it was important enough for him to spend his time on. He was too busy working to line his pockets with other people's money."

"You worked for him for a while. What was he like?"

"Distant, cold, smart."

"I understand he continued to perform his sheriff duties all during his trial."

"Right. There was no pressure from the people or the county commissioners for him to step down. He had the backing of Señor Fernando Dominguez who carried a lot of weight in Rio Arriba County. No one would dare have challenged the sheriff. It would have been considered disrespectful to Don Fernando."

"Don Fernando sounds like a powerful man."

"Oh, he is. I haven't met him personally but I've heard that no one gets a second chance to disrespect him. I've also heard that he's very loyal to his friends."

Rivera remained silent for the rest of the trip. Rio Arriba County was beginning to seem more like Mexico than New Mexico.

Gloria parked her unit and Rivera followed her into the sheriff's building. Sheriff Gallegos was sitting in his office, staring at the wall and taking a drag on a cigarette. Gloria knocked on the door and he waved them in. He opened his desk drawer and stubbed out his cigarette in the ashtray it contained. He exhaled a cloud of smoke.

"Sheriff, I thought you were trying to quit those things," said Gloria.

"I *am* trying." He shrugged. "This is only the third one today."

Gloria put her hands on her hips. "And besides, this is a no smoking facility."

He smiled. "That's why I keep the ash tray hidden in my desk." He dismissed the subject with a wave of his hand. "Anyway, how did Mrs. Archuleta take the news?"

"About like you'd expect," she said. "She was heartbroken."

He nodded. "That's understandable." Gallegos looked at Rivera. "What else can we help you with?"

"David Archuleta and Juan Baeza were shot and Victor Sanchez disappeared, all within a week. The three of them lived in Santa Elena and were close friends. That seems more than a little coincidental. What can you tell me about the Baeza shooting?"

"As I remember, it was accidental. I wasn't directly involved in the case. Let me dig out the case file and evidence box."

As Gallegos left his office, Rivera noticed Deputy Sheriff Gilbert Jaramillo had repositioned himself and was now sitting at an empty desk adjacent to the sheriff's office. Rivera wondered if he was motivated simply by curiosity or if he was spying on the sheriff at the behest of someone outside the department.

Gallegos returned with the case file and an evidence box, closed the office door, and sat down. He opened the file and read through it. "Let's see. The former sheriff handled this one. Baeza's body was found near Madera Canyon by a sheep herder. Apparently a couple of his sheep had wandered off from the flock and gotten lost. He happened upon the body about four hours after the shooting. The Medical Examiner said the cause of death was a .30 caliber bullet which struck Baeza in the back. That's a common round for hunting rifles around here. The report says there was no reason to suspect murder because Baeza had no known enemies. The sheriff decided it was a hunting accident." Gallegos looked up. "Except for a few photos of the crime scene and the ME's report, that's all that's in here."

Rivera couldn't believe what he was hearing. There had been no investigation at all. No interviews, no analysis, no theories formulated and tested. The hunting accident conclusion was just a guess. "Can I see the photos?"

"Sure." Gallegos pushed them across the desk.

Rivera studied them. They showed close-ups of Baeza's body from several different angles but there were no photos of the crime scene. No larger context within which to judge what might have happened. No crime scene tape appeared in any of the photos. Rivera handed them back to the sheriff. "Is the bullet in the evidence box?"

Gallegos pulled out a clear plastic bag containing the bullet and handed it to Rivera.

Rivera studied it. "David Archuleta was also killed with a .30 caliber bullet." He looked at Gallegos. "Maybe we should test the bullets for a match—see if they came from the same rifle."

"Why? You think maybe they were both killed by the same shooter?"

"Could be. It's worth checking."

"It's not likely—they were killed hundreds of miles apart—but I guess it couldn't hurt to check. Did you bring the slug from your shooting?"

"I brought everything—case file, evidence container, and the stuff I found in the Foster barn. It's all in my vehicle. I'll be right back."

Rivera extracted the materials related to the Archuleta case from his pickup, returned to the sheriff's building, and entered just as an elderly woman was leaving. She glanced at the items Rivera was carrying, gave him a fearful look, and scurried past him out of the building.

He set everything down on the table in the sheriff's office, and extracted the clear-plastic evidence bag containing the bullet that had killed Archuleta. Rivera compared the two bullets, side by side. "I can't be positive but the markings look similar. It's possible they were fired from the same rifle."

Gallegos came from behind his desk and looked over Rivera's shoulder. "I can have someone take them to the crime lab in Santa Fe. We'd have an answer by morning."

"Thanks, I'd appreciate that. Do you mind if I look through the evidence container?"

Gallegos gestured. "Help yourself."

Rivera picked through the clothing and personal effects found on Baeza's body. Shirt, cap, jeans, boots, socks, underwear. Several evidence bags contained the items from Baeza's pockets. Wallet, handkerchief, coins, and a pair of feathers. The feathers looked exactly like the ones Rivera had seen in the large cages behind the Baeza home and in the Foster workbench. He photographed them. Now he began wondering. What was the significance of the feathers? Feathers were something a bird lover like Baeza might carry, but why was Archuleta carrying them?

10

PATIENCE WAS NOT one of Rivera's virtues, especially when he was working on a murder case. But today, he had no choice—he'd have to wait until tomorrow to learn whether the two .30 caliber bullets were a match and to see if someone would be home at the Sanchez residence to answer his questions. Until then, there wasn't much else he could accomplish. He left the sheriff's building and headed for his vehicle, intending to check into his motel room. He'd been up since five o'clock in the morning and felt like he needed a hot shower and a good meal.

Gloria Valdez came running after him. "Are you hungry?" she asked.

"I was going to try to find a restaurant around here. Can you make a suggestion?"

"Meet me at the Three Ravens Coffee House in thirty minutes. It's got the best food in town but they close at four o'clock." She pointed down the street. "It's right over there. Fifteen minutes." She turned and left, not waiting for an answer. She hopped into her pickup and drove off.

Rivera smiled. He was used to getting a certain amount of attention from the ladies. He'd been kidded by the cops in Moab that many of the local women gawked at him when he walked through town. He was blessed with good looks—dark brown wavy hair, broad shoulders, and a handsome, friendly face. He'd suspected earlier in the day that Gloria had an interest in him as more than just a cop. It was the way she looked at him, studied his face, smiled. But maybe he was wrong. Maybe dinner would just be two cops getting together for some shop talk.

He looked in the direction Gloria had pointed and saw a gnarled cottonwood tree with three black raven sculptures sitting in its branches. Just beyond that was an old stucco building with a sign that read *Three Ravens Coffee House*. Rivera checked his watch. He was hungry. It seemed he was always hungry.

He drove to the Sundowner Motel, a place he'd found yesterday on the internet. There weren't many motels in Tierra Amarilla, and none had names he recognized, so he'd selected the Sundowner at random and made a guaranteed reservation. Now that he saw the place, he wished he'd made a better choice. It was an old motel out on the highway, a one story, U-shaped affair with about a dozen rooms wrapped around a gravel parking lot. It had whitewashed walls, a flat roof, and a flickering neon sign in the office window proclaiming there were vacancies. It looked like something right out of the 1950s.

A bony Anglo man with a long nose and thinning, combed-over hair glanced at Rivera as he walked into the office. He seemed annoyed at the interruption. He pushed a registration form across the counter without a word and returned his attention to a small television showing a black-and-white episode of *Gunsmoke.*

Rivera completed the registration process and walked to the door marked *10.* He inserted the key, pulled open the door, and was hit in the face with air that smelled stale and musty, as though the room had been closed up for a month. The room was small but it seemed to have everything he needed—a bed, a bathroom, a TV, a coffeemaker, and a wooden desk with a gooseneck lamp and a straight back chair. A small, noisy refrigerator sat in the corner with a microwave oven resting on top of it. Nothing fancy, just the bare essentials. He tested the mattress with his hand and found it acceptable—a little soft and saggy but not bad.

After he aired out the room, he unpacked, undressed, and turned on the shower. It took a full minute for the water to warm up, but the wait was worth it. The hot water running over his tired body seemed to relax and rejuvenate him. He dried off, ran a comb through his hair, and got back into his uniform, deciding to put on a fresh shirt. He checked his watch—he had a few minutes to sit and relax before heading over to the restaurant.

It had been a long day full of eye-opening surprises. Rio Arriba County was nothing like Grand County, Utah—and nothing like Las Cruces where he'd grown up. It seemed different in every conceivable way—the people, the culture, the landscape, the plant life, the legal system, the religious customs. Even the Spanish was different. The people in Santa Elena spoke with a Castilian accent, pronouncing the letters *z* and soft *c* like *th.* Rivera figured the community had been isolated in the mountains for so long that its residents still spoke the Spanish that the Conquistadors had taught their ancestors.

Rivera arrived at the Three Ravens Coffee House a few minutes early and parked in the lot behind the building. He walked past the wildflower gardens that flourished in a side yard, pulled open the front door, and stepped inside. The aroma of good food made him salivate. The restaurant could easily have passed for an upscale Santa Fe coffee house. It had polished wood floors and a high ceiling. Each table was surrounded with straight back chairs painted in multiple colors. The coffee and espresso equipment rivaled that of a Starbucks. He chose a table near a flaming gas fireplace, sat down, and perused the menu while waiting for Gloria. The restaurant served such fare as quiche, scones, panini sandwiches, salads, and cheeses. It was not what he'd expected to find in a town like Tierra Amarilla.

Gloria walked through the door ten minutes late, smiled, and waved. She had changed from her uniform into civilian clothes. Her long, shiny hair was down and she was wearing stretch jeans and a white blouse. Her deputy's uniform had kept hidden a stunning figure. Her earrings and necklace were silver and turquoise. She looked beautiful.

Rivera stood up and pulled out a chair for her. She gracefully slid into it.

"I decided to change clothes," she said. "This feels a lot better."

Rivera started to say it *looks* a lot better but stopped himself. He'd had enough experience with women to know a comment like that would lead to the inevitable question, *You mean I don't look good in my uniform?* And secondly, although he found her quite attractive, he was still committed to Amy. And now the thought of Amy gave him a stab of guilt for sitting here about to have dinner with this voluptuous green-eyed creature. He assuaged his guilt by telling himself he really didn't have a choice. Gloria had *instructed* him to meet her here.

They placed their orders. Gloria chose a salad with grilled chicken and a glass of chardonnay. Rivera ordered a roasted turkey sandwich with brie on a green chili croissant and a Miller Lite beer.

Gloria smiled. “Well, you had a long day, didn’t you?”

He nodded. “And an interesting one.”

“Do you really think the two shootings are connected?”

“We’ll know for sure tomorrow when we get the ballistics report. If the slugs were fired from the same rifle, then we’ve got two murders on our hands instead of just one.”

“I wonder what became of Victor Sanchez.”

“I don’t know, but I hope I can locate him. If I can question him, I’ll be able to learn a lot more about David Archuleta’s day-to-day activities. Right now, I have no idea what the motive for his murder was. And without understanding the motive, I don’t have much chance of finding his killer.”

“Let’s hope Victor wasn’t killed too.”

“Yeah, let’s hope so.” Rivera took a swig of beer. “Of course, it might turn out he’s our killer.”

Gloria nodded. “That thought had occurred to me.”

Rivera was curious about Gloria. She was beautiful and seemed smart and genuine. He wondered what she was doing in a place like Tierra Amarilla. “Are you originally from this area?”

“I was born in Cañones. It’s a small community hidden back in one of those canyons west of Abiquiu. We moved to Española when I was thirteen.”

"So you must know Rio Arriba County pretty well. How did you get into the law enforcement business?"

"My family didn't have much money, so when I graduated from high school, college was out of the question. I joined the Army so I could use the G.I. Bill to get a degree. I wanted to be a teacher. Then, much to my surprise and disappointment, the Army assigned me to a military police unit. I hated it at first. I had hoped I'd be assigned to some kind of training unit where I could get a head start on teaching. Funny thing was, I grew to like military police work and I enjoyed being around law enforcement people. I served one term in the Army and then enrolled at Northern New Mexico College in the Crime and Justice Studies program. After graduation, I served as a city cop in Colorado Springs for three years. That's where I met my former husband."

"Was he a city cop too?"

"No, he was a deputy sheriff." Her smile faded and she stared into her wineglass for a long moment, as if reliving events from her past. "The marriage was a disaster from the beginning—it lasted only six months. I guess he never outgrew being single. After work, he and his buddies would hit the bars and stay out late. Friends told me he was still chasing women. One night he came home drunk and smelling of perfume. When I called him on it, he slugged me." She pointed to her chin. "That's how I got this scar. I filed for divorce that week and then got an annulment from the Catholic Church. All I wanted was a normal marriage with a house and kids and neighbors. You know, a white picket fence and all that."

Rivera hated bullies, especially the kind that mistreated women. "Did you file assault charges against him?"

"No. I just wanted it to be over."

"Is that when you left Colorado Springs?"

"I left about a year later. I wanted to go back home so I could be closer to my parents. They were getting on in years and I didn't want to be too far from them. When the opportunity to become a Rio Arriba County deputy presented itself, I jumped at the chance. I'd heard all the stories about corruption in the county and about the sheriff's reputation for crooked dealings, but I came anyway. I rented a small house in Abiquiu, so now I'm only about an hour's drive from my parents." She smiled. "And here I am. So what's your story?"

"I grew up in Las Cruces with my two brothers and two sisters. I attended the UNM branch there and earned a degree in Criminal Justice. After that, I was a city cop in Las Cruces for four years. Then, about five years ago, I went to Moab and signed on as a Grand County deputy." He knew he should add something about his personal life. "I've never been married."

She smiled and held him with her green eyes. Took a sip of wine. "Why Moab?"

"When I was in high school, my senior class went on a bus trip up to Moab to see Arches National Park. I got hooked on that red rock canyon country as soon as I saw it. It just grabbed me and wouldn't let go. So as soon as I was offered a job in Grand County as a deputy, I grabbed it. My family and friends wanted me to stay in Las Cruces but I really wanted to experience life in the high desert. I miss them a lot so I visit every chance I get."

"Do you plan to spend the rest of your life in Moab?"

He laughed. "That's a question I'm wrestling with now."

"What do you mean?"

"Amy, the lady I'm dating, wants me to move to Albuquerque. She was just offered a job at the university there." Gloria lowered her wine glass to the table. He could see the disappointment in her face.

"So, is that something you're going to do?" she asked.

"I haven't had a lot of time to think about it. I just don't know."

"She's not willing to stay in Moab?"

"She's a PhD biologist and wants to work in a research university environment."

"How did you meet her?"

"The first time we met was at the Dolores River Research Institute in the backcountry east of Moab—it's a retreat facility for scientists on sabbatical. I was investigating the murder of a pothunter." He laughed. "The second time we met was in the middle of a shoot-out with some drug dealers."

She smiled. "I've heard shootouts are a great place to meet girls."

Rivera laughed. "After that, we started seeing each other on a regular basis."

"Are you engaged?"

"I don't know." Rivera hesitated. "Not formally, but I guess we were moving in that direction."

She reached over and patted his hand. "I'm sorry, I didn't mean to pry."

"No, that's okay. I wasn't sure how to answer because we're at a fork in the road in our relationship. With Amy talking about moving to Albuquerque, I don't know what's going to happen."

Gloria looked at her empty wine glass. "Want another before they close?"

"Sure. Why not?"

Gloria went to the counter and returned with a glass of wine and a beer. She sat down and raised her glass in a toast. "You could always move to T.A. and go to work here as a deputy. We need the help."

Rivera smiled. "I'd be a fish out of water here. Rio Arriba County is completely different from Grand County."

"What's so different?"

"Everything. The terrain, the culture, the people. You have Penitentes and Zapatistas and Dons. We have backcountry adventure seekers, Jeeps, and music festivals."

"Yeah. This is pretty much a traditional Hispanic community. I'm guessing there aren't too many Hispanics in Moab."

"There are some but it's mostly an Anglo community, like the rest of Utah."

"How long do you think that will last?"

"What do you mean?"

She laughed. "I have a theory about population demographics."

"Oh? What's that?"

"When the Europeans came to America, they killed off many of the indigenous peoples and subjugated the rest. Despite the cultural beliefs and rules of the various tribes, Native Americans were all forced to live under the white man's laws."

Rivera had no idea where this was going. "Yes, but back then, that kind of thing was going on all over the world. Colonizers had been invading and conquering new territories for all of recorded history."

"It was wrong and it was cruel. As best I can figure it, about a quarter of my blood is Native American, so I harbor a resentment of what the Europeans did when they came to the Americas." She smiled at him and raised her eyebrows. "But you see what's happening now. The Hispanic people in the U.S. are reproducing at a faster rate than the Anglos. Did you know that the population of California is now almost half Hispanic? Someday, we Hispanics will be a majority throughout the entire country."

Rivera shrugged. "So?"

She gestured. "Don't you see? It means the descendants of the conquered indigenous peoples will eventually reclaim their land using the white man's own laws." She laughed. "I think there's a delightful irony in that. With the passage of enough time, it seems to me that conquered peoples always slough off their conquerors."

Rivera had never heard an idea like that before. He wasn't sure he saw things that way, but he found Gloria's theory interesting. Of course, she seemed to be overlooking the three quarters of her blood that derived from the European conquerors. "I'd prefer to think we're all learning how to come together and live peacefully as one society."

"Maybe you're right. Anyway, we really could use some help in Rio Arriba County. If you hired on here, you'd be a lot closer to Albuquerque."

"Is there an opening?"

"The county commissioners have been discussing it. I think it might happen."

Rivera smiled. "That would give me an opportunity to work with Gilbert Jaramillo."

"Oh, Gilbert's harmless. When you get to know him, he's not so bad."

"I can't remember ever meeting a lawman like Jaramillo. The sheriff told me he was the nephew of Fernando Dominguez."

"Right. His employment is more of a favor to Don Fernando than anything else. Gilbert's mother was the Don's sister so, as a nephew of the Don, he gets to live in one of the houses on the estate. And, from what I hear, they're pretty nice houses."

"Well, I really don't know what the future holds for me. I've got to work all that out. But I'll add Rio Arriba to the list of possibilities."

Gloria smiled. "I would like that."

11

RIVERA ENTERED HIS motel room, turned on the lights, and closed the drapes. He stripped out of his uniform, and put on a faded Moab Music Festival T-shirt and some khaki shorts. He dialed Leroy Bradshaw's home number in Santa Fe.

A familiar voice answered the phone. "Hello."

"Sheriff Bradshaw, it's Manny Rivera calling."

"Well, hello, Manny. What a treat to hear from you. How are you doing?"

"Fine, Sir. How are you?"

"Great. I hope you're calling to tell me you're leaving Moab and coming to work for me in Santa Fe. I could sure use the help."

"I think about your offer often, especially when Sheriff Campbell goes on one of his tirades."

"You know, my biggest regret in leaving Moab was that Campbell would be elected sheriff. I hated to do that to the staff and the community, but after I lost Jill, I needed a change."

"The whole town would rejoice if you came back."

"I can't say I've never thought about it, but my business here is doing well, so I'll stay with it, at least for the time being. You know you have a job here whenever you want it, Manny."

Rivera didn't tell Bradshaw he'd actually been thinking about it. He didn't want any more pressure to leave Moab than Amy was already putting on him. "Thank you. I'll keep that in mind. Actually, I'm in New Mexico right now—in a motel in Tierra Amarilla. A cold case you'd be interested in led me here. Do you remember a young man who was murdered in the LaSal Mountains fifteen years ago? He was never identified, so the case was never solved."

"Sure, I remember. I was the investigating officer. That case has always bothered me—I couldn't make any headway on it. It was very frustrating. No one ever reported a missing person that matched the dead man's description. Have you been able to identify him?

"Yes. His name is David Archuleta. He was from a small village near Tierra Amarilla called Santa Elena." Rivera related the story Mrs. Foster had told him about her husband and described the items from Archuleta's backpack he'd found in the barn. Bradshaw, insightful as ever, probed Rivera with all the right questions. To Rivera, it seemed like old times. What a treat it was for him to be discussing a case with his mentor again.

They talked for twenty minutes about the Archuleta matter and relived a few old cases they'd worked on.

Rivera promised to keep Bradshaw informed on his progress. Before hanging up, Bradshaw made one last try at convincing Rivera to hire on. Rivera thanked him but remained noncommittal.

Rivera turned on the television and tried a few channels. The picture was fuzzy and distorted. He shut it off.

His thoughts drifted back to the Archuleta case. He'd been able to gather a few facts but the questions in his mind greatly outnumbered the answers. Two young men, friends from a small village in northern New Mexico, had been shot within days of each other, hundreds of miles apart. They had been friends since childhood, had gone to school together, and had done volunteer work in the community. They'd both had reputations as good citizens.

What else did they have in common? He thought for a long time. What about the feathers that Baeza was carrying in his pocket? Archuleta had carried the same kind in his backpack. Did the feathers have any meaning? Were they important to Rivera's case? He pulled out his iPhone and looked at the photo he had taken of the feathers in Foster's workbench. He expanded the image and studied it. The feathers were about six inches long with tan and dark brown stripes, exactly like Baeza's.

Using the Google app on his iPhone, he searched several websites related to birds and bird feathers. There were dozens of sites, most of them tailored to bird watchers or ornithologists. It didn't take him long to identify the feathers. They were clearly tail feathers from a great horned owl.

Rivera knew owls were prominent in Hispanic folklore. He remembered the warning his mother would give him when he was a young child playing outside the house with his friends. "Stay near the house or *La Lechuza* will get you." Fear of the great owl kept the kids from straying too far.

But these were real owl feathers and Archuleta and Baeza had been adults. Rivera considered that and remembered the cages in Baeza's backyard. Was there some larger picture suggested by the owl feathers and the cages? It was then that the idea struck him. Maybe the two young men had been in the owl poaching business. He knew that poaching certain birds was a felony and he was reasonably sure owls were included. But why poach owls? Was there a market for them?

He dialed Ronny Sampers, an old friend who had retired from the Utah Division of Wildlife Resources twenty years ago and who lived in Moab. He was in his eighties, but his mind was still sharp. Rivera had been on a few hikes with Sampers and knew his knowledge of backcountry wildlife was second to none. After the preliminaries and without going into all the details of the case, Rivera asked him about great horned owls.

"It's a federal crime to poach owls, Manny. A felony. There's a little-known law called the Migratory Bird Treaty Act which makes it a felony to possess, sell, or buy certain birds, their parts, their nests, or their eggs. Lots of bird species are covered by that law, and the great horned owl is one of them. Since feathers are bird parts, it's a felony to carry them or even pick them up off the ground."

"You're kidding, Ronny. You mean if a kid comes across a feather in the woods and he picks it up, and it happens to be from a bird that's on the list, he's committed a felony?"

Sampers laughed. "That's right, Manny."

"How many different birds are on that list?"

"Over a thousand."

Rivera couldn't believe what he was hearing. "How could the kid possibly know if the feather he found is from a bird on that list?"

"He probably couldn't. It's another one of those laws passed by Congress that's well-intentioned but not very sensible. Every kid in the world will pick up an interesting feather if he finds one. He'll take it home, show it to his parents, then bring it to school the next day and show it to his friends. The reason for writing the law in the first place was to join the international community in protecting migratory birds. It does protect them but maybe the language goes a little too far." He laughed.

"As far as I know, no kid has ever been arrested for picking up a feather."

"I've only seen one great horned owl in the LaSals and I've been up there hundreds of times. Would that be a good place for poachers to operate?"

"Well, you're lucky you saw that one. They're nocturnal birds and do most of their hunting at dusk or night time. You might hear them but you'd rarely see them. And yes, the LaSals would be a good place to poach owls."

"What about the mountains in northern New Mexico?"

"They would be good too. So would almost any other place in the country. Great horned owls range all across the U.S., Mexico, and Canada."

"So how would a poacher catch them?"

"It's not hard. A cage with live bait such as a rodent or a chicken fastened inside would attract them. The owl enters the cage and a spring-loaded door slams shut. Simple as that. But only a coldhearted person would do it."

"Why would anyone poach owls? Do they make good pets?"

"Not as far as the owl is concerned. Owls don't have flocking instincts like most birds. They're solitary creatures who bond only with their mates and their offspring. Any other creature is perceived either as a threat or as prey. Owls are not like, say, parrots—they have a flocking instinct. That's why they and most other birds, if caged, will bond with their human captor. Owls are beautiful to look at but since they don't have a flocking instinct, they would detest anyone who caged them."

"Is there a market for owls?"

"I understand there is, but I don't know much about that end of the business."

Rivera thanked Sampers, told him he'd buy him a beer when he got back to Moab, and clicked off. Then he searched the internet for sites advertising birds for sale. There were many. He narrowed the search for owls specifically and found a few sites, all of them overseas. He located a site in Great Britain selling great horned owls for a couple of hundred pounds each, less than three hundred dollars.

Was it possible Archuleta went to Moab to explore the LaSals in search of owls? Was he in business with Baeza capturing and selling owls? He thought about that for a long time, trying to make sense of it. Baeza had the cages behind his home and his mother revealed that, at one time, they were filled with birds. But why go all the way to Moab to poach owls when they can be found in New Mexico?

Besides that, Archuleta had no cage with him, although that could have been stolen too. Or left somewhere. But even so, why travel all the way to Moab to trap an owl that would bring less than three hundred dollars when they were available in New Mexico? Since

Archuleta and Baeza were both carrying owl feathers, maybe there was a market for the feathers too. But how much could a feather bring? The question answered itself—probably not much. Rivera's owl poaching theory was beginning to disintegrate.

Out of curiosity, he searched the internet for the list of birds covered by the Migratory Bird Treaty Act. He was amazed to find robins, sparrows, grackles, and blue jays included on the list. He'd seen thousands of them in the backcountry around Moab and everywhere else. He wondered why they were considered endangered. No explaining Washington, he thought.

Rivera was tired and his thinking was getting fuzzy. He decided to call it a day.

Before hitting the sack, he dialed the hospital in Moab and asked for the head nurse.

"Please tell Mrs. Faye Foster that the name of the young man who was killed in the LaSals fifteen years ago was David Archuleta and that I've informed his mother about his death."

"I'm sorry, Deputy Rivera, Mrs. Foster passed away early this morning."

Rivera thanked the nurse and clicked off. A vague feeling of emptiness enveloped him as he turned out the light and climbed into bed. Mrs. Foster had died without ever knowing he'd kept his promise.

12

RIVERA'S FIRST DISAPPOINTMENT the next morning came when he discovered the coffee maker in his motel room was out of order. He enjoyed a cup of coffee first thing in the morning but today he would have to wait. His second disappointment came when he arrived at his pickup and saw that someone had attached some kind of voodoo figure to the door handle. It was made of wax and dressed in what appeared to be a homemade deputy sheriff's uniform. A roofing nail had been stuck through the figure's midsection.

Rivera scanned the motel parking lot and saw no one. Perhaps it was just a prank. A sheriff's vehicle from Utah might make a good target for a mischievous youngster. But he knew better—it was no prank. More likely it was a message warning him that his presence in Rio Arriba County was not appreciated. He placed the figure in the center console of his vehicle and drove to the Three Ravens Coffee Shop.

He ordered coffee, chorizo, eggs with green chili, and corn tortillas, and sat at the same table he'd shared with Gloria. It was a cool morning and the gas fireplace provided a welcome warmth. The restaurant was busy but not too crowded. He compared it to the Rim Rock Diner in Moab where he ate breakfast each morning. It was similar in many ways—the smell of bacon and pancakes as soon as you opened the door, good food, warmth, locals chattering about the weather and politics. The only thing missing was Betty, the waitress who brought him his breakfast each morning. She was fifty-something, married four or five times, and always wore a too-tight white uniform with an exposed cleavage. Her bleached blond hair was piled haphazardly on top of her head and her outrageous flirtations directed at Rivera often made him blush. He missed that. Breakfast without Betty just wasn't the same.

Rivera arrived at the Sheriff's Office around eight thirty and found Deputy Sheriff Gloria Valdez waiting for him with a cup of hot coffee. She presented it to him with a smile as he sat down in the visitor's chair next to her desk. Gloria was wearing a little more eye makeup than she'd worn yesterday and Rivera detected a faint scent of lavender.

He glanced at the sheriff's office and saw it was empty. "Sheriff's not in this morning?"

"No. He called and said he had to take his wife to the doctor. Said he'd be in around noon."

"Any word from the crime lab on those two slugs?"

She shook her head. "Nothing yet. We should hear something by early afternoon. Have you had any more thoughts about a motive for Archuleta's murder?"

"I'm not sure it has any meaning, but the feathers found in Baeza's pocket looked exactly like the feathers in one of the large cages behind his house."

Gloria stared at Rivera. "How is that significant?"

"Archuleta was carrying the same kind of feathers in his backpack." Rivera explained that he'd found the feathers in the workbench drawer and that he'd mistakenly thought they'd come from the birds nesting in the barn. "It turns out those feathers are from great horned owls. I wondered last night if Archuleta and Baeza might be poaching owls and selling them."

"So? Is that illegal?"

Rivera couldn't restrain himself from showing off a little. "It's a felony to possess, buy, or sell birds protected by the Migratory Bird Treaty Act. That includes great horned owls. So Baeza was clearly breaking the law by capturing and caging those owls. It's even a felony to possess their feathers."

"Really? I had no idea. Around here, it's not unusual for kids to capture birds and keep them as pets. Most people couldn't afford to buy one in the pet store. Besides, capturing them gives the kids something to do. It's fun."

Rivera smiled. "Have you done it?"

"Absolutely. We did it when we were kids." She laughed. "Are you going to arrest me? Put me in handcuffs?"

He grinned. "Just a warning this time."

"So you're thinking maybe they had a little business on the side—selling owls to supplement their income?"

"I don't know how else to explain the feathers. It's possible Archuleta was up in the LaSal Mountains on a poaching mission."

"Are there great horned owls in the LaSals?"

"Yes. There are some problems with that theory, though."

"Like what?"

"First of all, the prices on the internet for a great horned owl run less than three hundred dollars apiece. Going to Moab seems like a lot of work and effort for not too much money."

"Yes, but the people living in villages like Santa Elena are poor. A few hundred dollars from time to time would be a nice supplement to their incomes."

Rivera nodded. "True."

"And don't forget, since importing owls would be illegal and risky, maybe the going price from a supplier here in the States is higher."

"Good point." Rivera liked the way Gloria's mind worked. "There's another problem, though. Why did Archuleta go all the way to Utah to trap an owl? He could just as easily have found one here in the

Tusas Mountains. They can be found anywhere in the country."

She nodded. "I see what you mean."

"And there's a third problem. Archuleta didn't have any trapping equipment with him. No cage, no bait. So how could he catch an owl in the LaSals?"

Gloria thought for a long moment. "You know, Manny, even if we had the answers to all those questions, there's still one overarching question. Assuming they *were* in the owl poaching business, why would anyone risk prison by killing owl poachers? Why not just turn them in and let the authorities handle it?"

"Good questions. Could be the killer was some kind of radical environmentalist who hated owl poachers." He shrugged. "Or maybe it was just personal. Anyway, I have a lot more digging to do. I need to go back to Santa Elena today and interview the Sanchez family. I'd like to find their son Victor and see what I can learn from him. Got plans for the day?"

"I'm in court this morning. I'd love to go with you, but I'm not sure when I'll be available."

Rivera refilled his coffee cup, left the Sheriff's Office, and headed for his vehicle. Sheriff Gallegos had recommended that he not go to Santa Elena alone, but he had no alternative. He certainly wouldn't want Gilbert Jaramillo to accompany him.

13

RIVERA DROVE BACK to Santa Elena under a dark blue sky populated with bright-white cumulus clouds. He was surprised at how much the countryside of Rio Arriba County appealed to him. He was used to the vast open landscape of southeast Utah where geologic formations of diverse colors and shapes were the predominant features. There, sediment layers had been carved and shaped by wind, water, gravity, and the passage of time, creating incomparable sandstone sculptures with strata of red, pink, white, gray, yellow, brown, and even green. Red rock canyons, rivers, arches, and buttes drew visitors by the thousands to photograph the natural wonders. Because the vegetation was sparse, there was little to obstruct the view. From the top of a mesa, one could see eighty miles or more. He had once pointed out to a visitor from the east coast who mocked the high desert for its lack of tall trees that, in the red rock canyon country, trees would just block the view.

The countryside around Santa Elena was different in countless ways. Tall trees, rugged mountains, and high valleys dominated the view and, because of the trees, one could rarely see farther than a couple of miles—but here, the trees were an important part of the view. This was a land of forested hills and mountains, interspersed with open fertile valleys and crystal-clear creeks. The scenery was growing on him.

Rivera parked in front of the Sanchez residence, noticing a dusty pickup parked alongside the house. The vehicle, which wasn't there yesterday, was an older model Ford with rosary beads hanging from the rear-view mirror and a religious statue fastened to the dashboard.

The house was modest and typical of Santa Elena—adobe brick construction with a stucco finish and a corrugated metal roof. The window frames and front door were painted turquoise. A tin crucifix hung above the door and a two-foot high statue of Saint Francis of Assisi stood in the front yard encircled by rose bushes.

Rivera knocked and waited. A thin man in his sixties with wavy salt-and-pepper hair opened the door. He adjusted his glasses, peered at the deputy's badge, and produced a slight frown.

"Yes, can I help you?" He spoke in Spanish.

"Are you Mr. Sanchez?"

"Yes."

Rivera introduced himself, explained he was investigating the murder of David Archuleta, and said he would like to ask Mr. Sanchez a few questions.

Sanchez stood frozen. "A few questions about what?"

"I'm trying to learn as much as I can about David."

Sanchez, supporting himself with a homemade cane, nodded for Rivera to come inside, displaying some reluctance as he did. The living room area was small and warm, furnished with a well-worn red couch and mismatched overstuffed chairs. A familiar smell Rivera recognized as freshly-made tamales filled the home. Mr. Sanchez shooed a small, brown dog off the couch and motioned for Rivera to sit there.

Sanchez introduced his wife, his daughter, and his granddaughter who were preparing tamales in the kitchen. The wife was short and pretty, wearing a flowery housedress and an apron. The daughter, Victor's sister, was slim and striking, about thirty-five years old. The granddaughter, whose name was Rosita, looked cute as a button with her hair fixed in a ponytail. She had her mother's face. Rivera guessed her age at six or seven. They were polite but reticent, said hello, and resumed their kitchen duties.

The dog walked over to Rivera, sniffed the cuff of his pants, and wagged his tail tentatively. Rivera rewarded him with a scratch behind the ears. Seemingly satisfied that Rivera was no threat, the dog trotted into the kitchen and began playing with Rosita.

Rivera surveyed the room. There were no modern conveniences to be seen—no computer, no television, no DVD player. The only nod to modernity was a plain black telephone mounted on the wall of the entryway to the kitchen. Rivera's eyes fell on a framed photograph hanging on the wall behind Mr. Sanchez. It showed a young man dressed in a white shirt, a dark coat, and a tie. He wore a serious expression and had a jagged scar over his right eyebrow.

"We always wondered what happened to David Archuleta. He disappeared a long time ago," said Mr. Sanchez. "We never heard from him again. Last night his mother told us he was found dead in Utah. Shot and killed. Why would anyone shoot that fine boy?"

"That's what I'm trying to find out," said Rivera. "I understand David and your son Victor were close friends."

Now Sanchez appeared ill at ease. "Yes, they were friends."

"I'd like to speak with Victor about David. Do you know where I can find him?"

"I'm sorry to tell you that my son disappeared about the same time David did. One day he left and we never heard from him again. We worry a lot and hope that someday he'll come home."

Rivera pointed to the photograph hanging on the wall. "Is that a picture of Victor?"

Mr. Sanchez nodded solemnly. "That's our Victor when he was twenty-one."

Rivera wanted to be certain about the chronology of events. Victor Sanchez had disappeared about the same time Archuleta was murdered and Baeza was killed in a hunting accident. Could Sanchez have had a falling out with them? Had something gone terribly wrong between three lifelong friends?

"Did Victor disappear before or after Juan Baeza was shot?"

"It was about that same time. A few days later."

"Did he have anything to say about Baeza's death?"

"I just remember he was very sad. He didn't say much. A couple of days later, he was gone."

"Why do you think he left?"

Sanchez shrugged. "I don't know. I thought maybe he and David ran off together to see the world."

"And you have no idea where he is now?"

Sanchez shook his head, eyes on the floor. "No idea."

Rivera sensed that Mr. Sanchez wasn't being totally forthcoming. He decided to try to shake him up a little—maybe he could get him to open up. He waited to speak until the granddaughter, who was headed toward the front door with the dog, was outside the house with the door closed. "Mr. Sanchez, I've been working with the Rio Arriba County Sheriff's office on this case. Did you know that withholding information in a capital murder case is a serious crime?" Rivera waited for a reaction.

Sanchez leaned forward, the fingers of his hands twisted tightly together. "I've told you everything I know."

After several additional unsuccessful attempts at getting Mr. Sanchez to talk, Rivera finally got up, thanked the man, and left. Sheriff Gallegos was right—the people living in these small villages weren't apt to open up to a stranger.

Outside, Rivera saw Rosita playing with the dog. She threw an old tennis ball down the street which the dog darted after, retrieved, brought back to her, and dropped at her feet.

Rivera smiled. "Hi, Rosita"

She produced a shy grin. "Hi."

Rivera knelt on one knee and began petting the dog. "I have a dog too. What's your dog's name?"

"His name is Perrito. He loves to play ball." She picked up the ball. Perrito crouched, his tail wagging in anticipation. She threw it and Perrito took off in a sprint.

"Do you live here with your grandfather?

She smiled and nodded with obvious enthusiasm. "And my *abuela* and my mama."

"Do you know your uncle Victor?"

She thought, nodded.

"When was the last time you saw him?"

She looked a little confused. "I never see him. He doesn't come here. I only talk to him on the phone."

"Oh. Well, when was the last time you talked to him on the phone?"

"Last Christmas. He always calls on Christmas and Easter and my birthday."

"That's nice. And when is your birthday?"

"June first. I'll be seven."

"Well, Easter is this Sunday. Only five more days. You'll get to talk to him again soon. Do you know where he lives?"

She shrugged. "No."

"Rosita! Come inside!" Her mother was leaning out from a partially opened door. "Come in here right away!"

Rosita, with Perrito close behind, ran to her mother and disappeared behind a closed door.

Rivera walked to his vehicle. So Victor hadn't really disappeared. He was still in touch with his family. At least he was alive.

Standing across the street from Rivera's vehicle was a shriveled-up old woman dressed in black. She was leaning on a walking stick, watching him. He smiled, touched the brim of his hat, and nodded in her direction. She frowned at him with a wretched, malevolent glare, pointed at him with a gnarled finger, stuck out a vibrating tongue, and produced a frightful hissing sound.

He hopped into his pickup, started the engine, and drove off. The old woman had to be the *bruja* named Josefina that Gloria had told him about. He was certain she'd just given him a *mal ojo*. He tried to smile and shrug it off, but found he couldn't. He'd always told himself there was nothing to witchcraft, even though he'd grown up around many people who believed in it and were deathly afraid of witches and their curses. Now he wasn't so sure. The experience created a discomfort within him. He felt mildly nauseous.

14

RIVERA TOOK A SIP of coffee as he drove through the village. The coffee was cold but it seemed to settle his stomach. He managed a smile, embarrassed at his reaction to the *mal ojo.* He shook it off as best he could and tried to regain his objective composure. Of course witches had no power.

Rivera found himself becoming more and more interested in the people of Santa Elena and their hardscrabble life. They didn't have much, yet they had everything they needed—a home, a vehicle, food, clothing, family, friends, neighbors, and a church. They lived in a beautiful, fertile valley with a crystal-clear creek running through it. Upstream, small diversion dams had been built and irrigation ditches called acequias had been dug to supply water to the fields. He guessed the acequias, which were lined with rock, dated back to the earliest days of the village—probably they'd been built by the original settlers.

He didn't feel particularly welcome here, but that was understandable. Over the centuries, the people of Santa Elena had learned the hard way not to trust strangers. Outsiders were the ones who stole their land. He understood that getting these people to open up and give him the information he needed to break his case was going to be difficult. Nevertheless, he had no choice but to persist until he had the facts. Leroy Bradshaw had always counseled him: *First, make sure you get all the facts. Applying logic to an incomplete set of facts will always lead to an incorrect conclusion.*

He stopped in front of the village church. A black, dusty ATV was parked on the side of the building. Rivera had always found priests and other religious leaders to be good sources of general information about their communities. He decided to take a look inside the church on the chance that the ATV belonged to the local priest. Maybe he could help Rivera understand how to connect better with the people.

The front door was massive for such a small church. It was made of heavy pine slabs with a hand-carved image of the Blessed Virgin imbedded in its face. He pulled on the wrought iron handle, but the door wouldn't budge.

He circled around to the back of the building and found the rear door ajar. He entered, waited for his eyes to adjust to the dim light, and took a seat in the front pew. The altar was small with a white linen cloth draped over it. On each side was a tall candle in a brass candleholder. Behind the altar was a large wooden cross with a Jesus figure nailed to its beams. Blood dripped from his hands, feet, and side, and from the crown of thorns on his head. To the right of the altar was a statue of the Blessed Virgin, an array of red votive candles at her feet. Stations of the Cross depictions were painted on the walls. The smell of candle wax and incense triggered memories of Rivera's earlier years as an altar boy.

Rivera grew up Catholic and still considered himself a Catholic, but wasn't rigorous in adhering to the rules. He frequently missed church on Sunday and hadn't been to confession in years. Those were little facts he'd never want his mother to learn.

He knelt, crossed himself, and said a few Hail Marys. His reason for praying wasn't because that's what a Catholic was supposed to do in church. Oddly, he prayed because it made him feel as though someone had his back.

A noise in the rear of the church interrupted his thoughts. He turned his head and saw an elderly man mopping the floor of the vestibule. Rivera approached him, introduced himself, and asked where he could find the priest.

"The priest only comes here on Sunday. Mass is at ten o'clock."

"He doesn't live in Santa Elena?"

"Oh, no. Our village is too small to have its own priest. Father Maclovio visits us from his parish in Española. He brings the sacraments to several small villages in the mountains every Sunday. He is a good man. A saint."

"You're lucky to have him," said Rivera, trying to keep the conversation going.

"Oh, yes, I know. For many years, we had no priest. We had a church but no one to bring us the sacraments. Then Father Maclovio began coming to our village."

"What did you do before he started coming?"

"Before that, all we had was the Penitentes. They tried to fill the void with their prayers and good deeds."

"When did Father Maclovio start coming?"

"Oh, I think it was ten or eleven years ago."

"Are the Penitentes still active?" Rivera remembered that David Archuleta was a Penitente. Perhaps they would be another source of information.

"Oh, yes. They have been here since the village was founded. They have about a dozen members. Like all Penitente brotherhoods, they are very secretive. But they are helpful and generous to the community. They have a private meeting place. A *morada.* It's up on the hillside just past the cemetery."

"Do you think anyone would be there now?"

"I don't know. You could try. Señor Abelardo Herrera, the man who is chief of the *cofradía,* is often at the *morada* working. There's a dirt road next to the church that leads up to it."

15

RIVERA STARTED HIS engine, turned onto the rutted dirt road leading to the *morada,* and slowly drove upslope. Halfway up the hill, he saw a grassy lane on his left which led to a cemetery surrounded by a two-foot high rock wall. A wrought iron arch over the entrance displayed the words *Camposanto Santa Elena.* The gate was open, so Rivera, curious to see what a graveyard in an old Hispanic village looked like, detoured into the cemetery and got out of his pickup. The air was fresh and cool, and the sun warmed his face and shoulders. Small pink and yellow flowers were in bloom. His nostrils detected a faint scent of pine.

He studied the gravestones. Some were new and polished, others old and roughhewn as though they'd been shaped with a chisel and mallet. Each grave, regardless of its age, was decorated with colorful plastic flowers. Some of the gravesites had statues of Christ, the Blessed Virgin, a favorite *santo,* or a large crucifix. Many family plots had perimeters of wrought iron fencing. He recognized some of the names on the gravestones: Archuleta, Baeza, Sanchez.

The Archuleta portion of the cemetery contained over two dozen markers. The oldest was the gravesite of Candido Archuleta who was born on March 16, 1810 and died on June 7, 1876. By Candido's side was the grave of his wife Agueda. Those gravesites were also decorated with colorful plastic flowers. The descendants of Santa Elena's old ones never forgot to pay homage to their ancestors.

There was something about old graveyards that had always attracted Rivera. Passing through small towns, he would often stop and visit the local cemetery to read the inscriptions on the gravestones. It was a way of learning about the community and its history. One time, in the cemetery of a small, predominantly Mormon town in Utah, he came upon a gravestone that was about a hundred years old. On the front of the stone was a man's name along with the dates of his birth and death. On the back of his gravestone was a list of his six wives. Two of the wives had been sisters. It was noted that he'd had forty-one children.

Cemeteries had a way of putting life into perspective for Rivera. Sooner or later, everyone ended up dead. For him, that added a sense of urgency to his time on earth. There was a firm deadline for everything he wanted to accomplish, and for Rivera, getting married and having a family was high on the list. Amy Rousseau was supposed to be part of those plans. Now he wasn't so sure.

Cemeteries also forced him to confront another question. When he died, would anyone visit his grave, remember him, and leave flowers?

Rivera shaded his eyes and looked out over the landscape. What a beautiful setting for a cemetery, he thought. The descendants of its occupants lived in the village below, and the whole community was nestled in forested hills and mountains. There was a profound silence, except for a few birds chittering as they hunted for seeds amongst the gravestones. A horse whinnied in a distant field. Santa Elena was a peaceful place—Rivera began wondering if he could be happy living in a village like this.

He returned to his pickup, left the cemetery, and continued up the dirt road toward the *morada*. It was a small L-shaped building, constructed of gray clapboards and a shingled roof with a single cross on top. There were small windows high on the walls, beyond the reach of curious eyes, yet large enough to allow light to illuminate the interior.

Rivera pulled into a dirt parking area next to the *morada*. He spotted two men standing behind the building, talking to each other and watching him. Both appeared to be in their sixties. One was a stocky man with beautiful white hair, the other a tall, slender man holding a rake. Behind them was a life-sized statue of Christ garbed in a white robe with a red sash, hunched over and carrying a cross. Farther up the hill were three large crosses. Rivera got out of his pickup and strolled over to the men. He introduced himself and asked where he could find the chief of the *cofradía.*

The stocky man responded. "I am Abelardo Herrera and I have the honor of serving as chief of our *cofradía.*" He gestured toward the other man. "And this is Flaco Chavez, one of our members." Chavez nodded silently, then moved away from them and began raking the area, though there was little grass there. He seemed to be raking mostly dirt.

"I'm a deputy sheriff from Grand County, Utah, and I'm investigating a homicide that took place up there a long time ago. I'm working with the Rio Arriba County Sheriff. I wonder if I might ask you a few questions."

The man looked around with exaggerated wide eyes and a mock craning of his neck. "Where is the Rio Arriba County Sheriff? I don't see him." Then he looked at Rivera, grinned, and waited.

Now Rivera wished he hadn't said he was working with the local sheriff. He was trying to subtly establish his authority, of which he had none, but the *cofradía* chief saw right through it and politely let him know. "He and the deputy I'm working with had appointments this morning. I'm here alone and I hope I can count on your cooperation. If necessary, I can wait until the deputy arrives this afternoon. I'm seeking information about David Archuleta. He was murdered in my county fifteen years ago."

"Yes, I know."

"You know?"

"Of course, Señor." He smiled. His perfect white teeth contrasted with the brown skin of his face. "You informed his mother yesterday. By now, everyone in Santa Elena knows."

Rivera felt a bit silly. In a village of 300 people, of course everyone would know by now. "I understand he was a Penitente in your *cofradía*."

Herrera's gaze dropped from Rivera's face and now he looked at the ground, apparently considering how he would respond. *Cofradías* were secret societies and Rivera had the feeling Herrera was deciding how much, if anything, he wanted to reveal to this interloper. Herrera nodded. "Yes, David was one of our members. At this *morada* and also at the old *morada* in the forest. We built the new one here about seventeen years ago so we would be closer to the village."

"I'm trying to learn as much as I can about him. Someone had a reason to kill him and if I can figure out the reason, maybe I can figure out who did it."

Herrera shrugged. "I can't think of a single reason anyone would want to kill him. David was a fine young man. He was a gentle soul who helped the less fortunate in the village. That's what the Penitente movement is all about. We receive a lot of criticism because we're secretive and our prayers and rituals are done privately in the *morada*. But we are also dedicated to helping the people of our community. Are you familiar with the Penitente movement?"

"Only generally. I don't know as much as I should. I'd like to know more."

"Then allow me to enlighten you. We are known more formally as the Brotherhood of Jesus of Nazareth. We are a religious organization dedicated to honoring Jesus Christ and adhering to the principles he espoused. Our history goes as far back as the thirteenth century in Europe. The Penitentes came from Spain to America with Don Juan de Oñate in the late 1500s. Some *cofradías* worked their way north from Mexico to New Mexico, arriving in Rio Arriba County in the late 1700s. The villages here were too small and isolated to be formally served by the Catholic Church. There were very few priests and churches, so it fell on the members of the brotherhood to fill the void. We serve the community with lay services, penance, and good works. Our *cofradía* is small—only a dozen members—but we are very active. This Friday is Good Friday, an important day for the Penitentes. We will have our annual procession from the *morada* to the place in the mountains we call *El Calvario.* The ceremony pays homage to Christ's crucifixion and death."

Rivera had heard about the Penitentes' processions but had never seen one. "Are non-members allowed to view the procession?"

"Yes, of course. Non-members are welcome at our processions. Our secrecy is limited only to the activities which take place inside the *morada.* Because of our secrecy, uninformed people tend to sensationalize our rituals and overlook the good deeds we do in the community. They refer to us as an evil cult and ascribe dark motives to our private meetings. Nothing could be farther from the truth. The Knights of Columbus have their secrets; so do the Masons; so do many university fraternities. Like them, our secrets help bind us together." He smiled. "The Catholic Church banned us as dangerous extremists for centuries, but in the 1950s they finally decided we were no threat. We feel we exemplify how Christians should lead their lives. We're all about giving to the community and doing penance for our sins and the sins of others. David Archuleta was a perfect example of a devout Penitente. He would have given away his last penny if someone in Santa Elena needed it."

Finally, Rivera had found someone in the village willing to talk to him. He was relieved and a little surprised that Herrera seemed open to answering his questions. Rivera figured it was only because the victim had been a member of Herrera's *cofradía.* "Were Juan Baeza and Victor Sanchez also Penitentes?"

"No. Just David. But the three of them were best friends. They were always together, ever since they were old enough to walk. They were fine young men and as different as can be. David was a poet and nature lover type, Juan was an athlete, and Victor was a scholar. Juan was killed in a hunting accident and Victor left Santa Elena long ago."

"Can you think of anyone David had a problem with? Anyone at all?"

"No. When I learned last night he was murdered, I couldn't believe it. He was honest, polite, generous, and wouldn't hurt a soul. It's a mystery to me. I hope you find the one who did it and punish him."

Rivera had a sinking feeling that he might never identify the motive for Archuleta's killing. Everyone loved him—he sounded like a saint. "What kind of things did David do in the community?"

"All three of those boys were enterprising and worked various jobs in the community. Construction, farming, ranching, you name it. As I recall, they also held part-time jobs working for the highway department. David was their leader. They always seemed to have money and spent most of it on community projects and assisting individuals in need—food for Mrs. Atencio and her four kids, medicine for Mr. Marques, school supplies for whoever couldn't afford them. One summer, they rebuilt the church steeple. They organized sports events for the kids, mentored the ones having trouble in school, and even taught English to anyone who wanted to learn it. They epitomized the purpose of the Penitentes."

"David had lash marks on his back when he was found. Was that from self-flagellation?"

"Yes. He was a flagellant. He lashed himself often and especially during Holy Week. It's an extreme form of penance."

Rivera was interested in the *morada* and couldn't suppress his curiosity. "Any chance I could peek inside the *morada*?"

Herrera laughed. "Sure. We don't encourage visitors and we certainly don't allow them to come to our meetings. Today some of our members are inside planning the Good Friday procession. I guess it wouldn't do any harm to let you have a look through the back door into one of the rooms." He opened the door a few inches and allowed Rivera to peer inside.

There wasn't much to see—benches around the perimeter of the room, a podium, and a large crucifix. Three men were sitting around a wooden table talking. After a few seconds, Herrera closed the door.

"It's a pretty minimal building," said Rivera. "What was the old *morada* like?"

"It was smaller and even more basic than this one, but the view from the old *morada* was breathtaking. Now, of course, it's abandoned. You might want to check out the view up there before you leave."

"Where is it located?"

"It's on a hillside at the base of the mountains, overlooking Estaca Canyon where that young girl from Canjilon committed suicide a long time ago. She jumped off the bluff and fell to her death. Some said she'd been cursed by a *bruja*. Others said she just went crazy. Anyway, as a result, people don't go there much anymore. They think that area is cursed." Herrera pointed toward the forest. "If you want to see the view, follow that dirt road to the end. It's a little over a mile to the old *morada*."

16

RIVERA LOOKED AT his watch. It was noon and he was anxious to meet with the sheriff as soon as possible—he wanted to know whether the two slugs sent to the crime lab were a match. Seeing the view at Estaca Canyon would have to wait for another day. He drove out of the mountains back toward Tierra Amarilla, enjoying the beauty of the landscape despite the persistent nausea he felt.

He entered the sheriff's office and scanned the area. Gloria Valdez was back in the office, Ruby was busy at her word processor, and Gilbert Jaramillo was sitting at his desk eyeing Rivera. Unfortunately, the sheriff had not yet returned.

A small, elderly woman was seated in front of Gloria's desk, silent and looking nervous. She was twisting her tightly intertwined fingers on her lap. He remembered seeing her in the office yesterday.

"Deputy Rivera, this is Señora Lujan," said Gloria. "She was here yesterday when you and I were talking to the sheriff. When you went to your vehicle and brought back the material from the Archuleta case, she saw something you were carrying that frightened her. She left without saying anything about it because she was scared, but today she came back to warn us."

Rivera smiled at the woman and bowed his head slightly, then turned his attention to Gloria. "What did she see that frightened her?"

"It was an item from Archuleta's backpack. She recognized it."

"*La Santa Muerte!*" the woman said in a hoarse whisper. "*La Santa Muerte!*" She rose from her chair and scurried out of the building with a fearful expression on her face.

Rivera looked at Gloria. "The Death Saint? What the hell is that?"

"She's referring to the figurine you found in the barn. When I saw it yesterday, I thought it was just a Day of the Dead carving, but Mrs. Lujan referred to it as a *santo.* In the Mexican culture, there are lots of different *santos,* each with its own purpose. They're very popular in New Mexico as I'm sure you know. Catholics revere them and display them in their homes. Each one has a different purpose—health, good fortune, successful harvest, and so forth. The *santeros* who carve them from cottonwood roots are considered artists. But I've never seen this particular *santo* before. I'm not sure what its purpose is."

"I'll go fetch it from the container. Maybe we can find someone to enlighten us."

When Rivera had first seen the *santo* in the Foster barn, he hadn't paid much attention to its details. Like Gloria, he'd figured it was just another Day of the Dead figurine. Now he studied her more closely. *La Santa Muerte* was a six-inch-tall skeletal figure clad in a black, hooded robe. Each eye socket of her skull was filled with an aquamarine colored bead. She wore a jeweled crown on her head, and around her neck hung several beaded necklaces. In one of her skeletal hands, she held a scythe giving her a kind of grim reaper image. In her other hand was a crystal ball. Rather than being hand carved from a cottonwood root, the body of the figure was made from a heavy resinous material poured into a mold—a less expensive process.

Gloria looked at the *santo*. "Kind of creepy looking."

"Yeah. Now we have to find out if it has any significance."

She seemed mildly surprised by Rivera's comment. "What for?"

Rivera had never liked loose ends. On one of his cases when he was a less experienced deputy, he'd allowed a seemingly minute detail to slide by without taking the time to thoroughly understand it. That instance of intellectual laziness had turned out to be a big mistake, unnecessarily delaying his investigation several days and almost allowing a killer to escape. He'd broken that bad habit and now, in his investigations, he delved into every detail until it made sense to him. "I've learned that when you don't know what's important and what isn't, it's a good idea to treat *everything* as important. Who knows? This *santo* might help explain what Archuleta was doing in the LaSals."

She nodded with a doubtful expression. "Okay. Well, there's a *santero* I know who lives in Los Ojos, just a few miles from here. We could drive over there and see if he's familiar with it."

"Good idea. Let's go."

Gloria drove while Rivera took in the sights. As they descended a hill into the village of Los Ojos, he spotted an enormous rock grotto on the side of the road. It was situated partway up a hillside and contained a statue of Our Lady of Lourdes. A smaller statue depicted a young girl praying at her feet. Colorful plastic flowers had been left by visitors to the site.

"There sure are a lot of grottos around here."

"The locals revere the Blessed Mother and the saints. Their belief in the teachings of the Catholic Church is strong."

They drove into the small village, parked in front of the *santero's* shop, and went inside. The scent of freshly cut wood reminded Rivera of the workshop in his backyard where his father used to make mesquite vases and bowls as a hobby. The *santero* looked up from an electric sander, saw Gloria, and smiled. He was a small man with a round face, thick rimless glasses, and calloused hands. The front of his shirt was covered with sawdust. He turned off the sander and put down the piece he was crafting, an eighteen-inch figure of a saint Rivera didn't recognize. The *santero* wiped the sawdust off his glasses with his sleeve and greeted Gloria like an old friend.

"Welcome back, Deputy Valdez. It's so good to see you again. Have you returned to buy some more of my wife's *pan dulce*?"

She laughed. "Oh no, Señor." She patted her stomach. "Too many of your wife's pastries and no man will ever look at me."

He grinned. "There's not much chance of that, Señorita, I can assure you. Even Señor Avila across the street enjoys looking at you when you come for a visit."

"Señor Avila? Why, he must be eighty years old."

"He's eighty-six. He told me one time that he still looks at women—he just can't remember why." The santero's face lit up and he let out a squeaky staccato laugh.

Gloria and Rivera laughed with him. She made the introductions and explained the purpose of their visit.

"Let me have a look at it," said the *santero.*

Rivera handed him the *santo.* "Anything you can tell us about this *santo* would be appreciated."

While the *santero* studied the *santo*, Rivera's eyes wandered around the shop. It was full of woodworking equipment—a band saw, a drill press, and several electric sanders, as well as a collection of knives, punches, files and awls on a workbench. Artist's paintbrushes and an array of paint cans filled a table against the wall. The floor was littered with sawdust and wood shavings. An assortment of gnarled cottonwood roots was piled in one corner. Shelves in the room were filled with colorful *santos* of many different designs and sizes. As his eyes scanned the shelves, Rivera wondered if there was a *santo* there that would help him work things out with Amy.

"It's *La Santa Muerte*," announced the *santero*. "The scythe and crystal ball in her hands make me certain. Some call her *Santisima Muerte*."

"I've never seen one like this before," said Gloria. "What is her purpose?"

"She is a folk saint very popular in Mexico. There is a large shrine devoted to her in Mexico City even though the Catholic Church denounces her as a satanic cult figure. In recent years, she has become popular north of the border. Her followers are people seeking protection from the evil that lurks in their lives. She helps to fend off wrongdoing from others or carry out vengeance against those who have done them harm. She is popular among small business owners, artists, and poor people—they build altars honoring her in their homes. She is also venerated by drug dealers. They seek her protection for their drug shipments and to ward off law enforcement."

Rivera and Gloria looked at each other. "Do you know which *santero* might have made this?" asked Gloria.

He looked at the floor and shook his head. "No."

"Anything else you can tell us about *La Santa Muerte*?" asked Rivera. "Anything at all?"

The santero looked at the statue and studied it. He shrugged. "No. Only that sometimes an owl is part of the carving. It would sit at her feet. But I don't see one here."

That reminded Rivera of the owl feathers carried by Archuleta and Baeza. "What about owl feathers?" he asked. "If someone carried owl feathers in his pocket, what would that signify?"

"I've heard that owl feathers, just like *La Santa Muerte*, are used to protect those in the illegal drug trade from law enforcement."

As they drove back to the sheriff's office, Rivera looked at Gloria. "Well, that was interesting. This casts a whole new light on things. Maybe this case isn't about owl poaching at all. Maybe it's about drug dealing."

17

RIVERA HELD OPEN the door as Gloria preceded him into the sheriff's building. His mind was adjusting to the concept of drug dealing as the underlying cause of the Archuleta killing. He was busy reshuffling the facts he'd gathered, attempting to see just how they might support such a conjecture.

Sheriff Gallegos was sitting at his desk, talking on the phone. While Rivera waited, he went to the water cooler, filled a paper cup, and drank it. High altitudes always made him thirsty.

Gallegos hung up the phone and gestured for Rivera and Gloria to come in.

"Any results from the ballistics analysis?" asked Rivera.

"I just finished talking to the crime lab," said Gallegos. "Your hunch was right. Both bullets were fired from the same gun."

Rivera sat down. "So that means Baeza's death was not a hunting accident."

"Yeah. Now we have two murder cases to solve. I guess this makes us partners."

"Since Archuleta and Baeza were killed by the same person, it's likely they were both killed for the same reason," said Rivera. He explained what he and Gloria had learned about *La Santa Muerte* and the owl feathers. "They may have been involved with illegal drugs."

Gallegos nodded. "That wouldn't surprise me. There's plenty of drug dealing going on around here. Rio Arriba County has one of the highest death rates in the country from people overdosing on heroin."

"Drug dealing looks like the logical place to start searching for a motive," said Rivera. He explained that he'd initially thought the case was related to owl poaching, but rejected that theory because the economics made no sense.

"What do we know about the two victims?" asked the sheriff.

"They both grew up in Santa Elena. They and their friend Victor Sanchez were close friends—buddies since childhood. From what I've been able to learn, the three of them were model citizens. They spent much of their time helping people in the community who needed assistance. Victor left Santa Elena years ago."

"Model citizens don't normally deal in drugs."

"The drug dealers I've dealt with are a hard and ruthless bunch, and these guys sound like Eagle Scouts.

Based on their reputations, they don't seem the type to be dealing, but I don't know what else to conclude."

"Did they have jobs?"

"They held various jobs in Santa Elena and occasionally worked for the highway department. A lot of their time was consumed by the volunteer work they did in the community."

"So who would want to kill them?"

Rivera shrugged. "I'd guess someone connected with the drug trade—a supplier, a customer, or maybe a competitor."

"Were they users themselves?" asked the sheriff.

"Not that I'm aware of. But I haven't actually asked that question."

"What about Victor Sanchez? Have you questioned him?"

"I spoke to his father. He said Victor disappeared right after the Baeza shooting and hasn't been seen since." Rivera noticed that Gilbert Jaramillo had repositioned himself close to the sheriff's office. He was pretending to be reading a file.

"Do you think Victor was dealing too?"

"It wouldn't surprise me."

"Any idea why he disappeared?"

"No, not with any certainty. He might have run because he feared for his life, or maybe he took off because he killed his two friends. We can't be sure. In any case, I guess we'd have to put Victor's name on the list of suspects."

Gallegos nodded. "If he's still alive. Maybe someone had reason to whack all three of them."

Rivera considered telling the sheriff what Rosita had said about her Uncle Victor's periodic phone calls, but rejected the idea. For that nugget of information to be of any benefit, the sheriff would have to request that a local judge issue a subpoena to the local telephone company to produce the phone records of the Sanchez residence. Based upon what Rivera had learned thus far about the inner workings of Rio Arriba County, everybody within a hundred miles would know within the hour. Rivera would lose whatever advantage he had in knowing that Sanchez was alive and well, without Sanchez being aware that Rivera knew. If Sanchez learned his secret was out, he might run again. Rivera wanted him to stay right where he was. He would try to obtain the information about Sanchez's whereabouts through some other channel. The search for him would be a delicate matter requiring care and secrecy. Besides, Jaramillo was listening to their every word and would be passing along the information to whomever he was reporting.

"So where do we go from here?" asked the sheriff.

Rivera thought for a moment. “I’m not sure. I’ll review everything tonight and visit with you in the morning. Maybe I’ll have an idea by then.”

As he left the office and headed for his vehicle, he noticed the queasiness in his stomach was still with him. Maybe a good meal would help settle it down.

18

THE HANDPAINTED LETTERING on the door said *Pete's Deluxe Dining Room.* Rivera pulled open the door and entered a small, dark room with a jukebox and a dozen tables. Faded pictures on the walls depicted scenes of farms, ranches, and antique automobiles. No other patrons were present and the jukebox was silent. The restaurant's name seemed a bit overstated to Rivera as he surveyed the place, but it was after four o'clock and the Three Ravens Coffee House was closed. Pete's would have to do.

He found a booth in the back corner and slid into the seat. An elderly waitress with a tired face and a detached manner brought him a menu and a set of utensils rolled up in a paper napkin. The menu was a single sheet of paper inside a slightly greasy plastic cover. He ordered the chicken enchilada plate and a Miller Lite.

The waitress returned with Rivera's beer and set it down on the table. He took a long swig and thought about calling Amy. He missed her and wanted to tell her about the progress he was making on the case. He wanted to get her feedback—and her approval. He pulled his cell phone out of his pocket and began punching in her number. Then he stopped. What would he tell her when she asked him about moving to Albuquerque? He had no idea—and right now he didn't want a long debate about why he should leave Moab. He literally didn't have the stomach for it. *If you really loved me, you would come with me,* she would say. And he wouldn't know what to reply. He dropped the phone back into his pocket.

He ate his meal, thinking the whole time about both the Archuleta case and his relationship with Amy, mentally toggling back and forth between the two topics, reaching no conclusions about either. It turned out that Pete's Deluxe Dining Room served up some pretty good food, but the meal had done nothing to settle the uneasy feeling in the pit of his stomach. He finished his beer, paid the tab, and left.

He stopped at a nearby convenience store and picked up a six-pack of Miller Lite. When he arrived back at the motel, he discovered a symbol had been drawn with a felt tip pen on the door to his room. It was a five-pointed star inscribed in a circle. Another act of witchcraft, he figured, becoming more convinced that someone was trying to either harm him or scare him off. He took a picture of the symbol with his iPhone and went inside.

He put the beer in the refrigerator and called Leroy Bradshaw at home in Santa Fe.

"Sheriff, I need a favor."

"Sure Manny, how can I help you? And, by the way, you can stop calling me 'Sheriff.' I'm not the sheriff any more. Call me Leroy."

Rivera produced a nervous laugh. "It's a hard habit to break. I always think of you as Sheriff Bradshaw. So does everyone else in Moab." Rivera wondered if he could ever call his old boss by his first name. Probably not. He had too much respect for him.

"So how can I help you?"

"Do you have any connections at the phone company?" asked Rivera.

"A man that works for me does. What do you need?"

"Someone calls the Sanchez residence in Santa Elena every Christmas, Easter, and June first. I need to know the source of those calls."

"What's June first?"

"It's a little girl's birthday."

"I take it this is urgent."

"Kind of. A murder took place in Rio Arriba County a couple of days after David Archuleta was killed in the LaSals. The victim's name was Juan Baeza. He was from the same village as Archuleta. The former sheriff, now in prison for a number of crimes, declared it a suicide without much of an investigation."

"Yeah, I've heard about that guy. He was bad news."

"Baeza was shot with a .30 caliber rifle. It turns out it was the same rifle that was used to kill David Archuleta."

Bradshaw whistled. "No kidding. That's real interesting. It sounds like you're making good progress on the case."

"Victor Sanchez, the man who makes the calls to Santa Elena, knew Archuleta and Baeza well. I need to find him and question him. Either he's our killer or he disappeared because he was afraid he'd be the next victim."

"I'll get right on it and call you back as soon as I have something."

"Thanks very much, Sheriff." Rivera hung up before Bradshaw could correct him again. The fact was, he didn't want to call his old boss "Leroy." He liked their relationship just the way it was. Bradshaw was the only genuine boss Rivera had, even if it was only in his mind. Certainly he didn't think of Denny Campbell as his boss. Campbell was more like an impediment, an irritant, a dark cloud hovering overhead. Rivera realized that, even now, he strove in his work to impress Bradshaw and meet his standards of excellence, even though Bradshaw no longer occupied the big office down the hall.

Rivera began thinking about what might have happened fifteen years ago when David Archuleta and Juan Baeza were killed and Victor Sanchez disappeared. He'd rejected the owl poaching theory for good reason.

The economics of such an operation didn't add up. The drug running theory made a lot more sense—and it probably involved all three friends.

That meant they had to have a supplier and a market. The supplier could have come from anywhere, but what about their market? Were these small villages in the mountains where the three men marketed their drugs? Possibly, but that question made him wonder how many of the residents could afford to buy drugs.

Assuming they were involved with drugs, what kind of drugs were they dealing? Since Archuleta was found dead in the LaSals, Rivera wondered if this could be another case of growing marijuana on public lands. He had broken such a case a few years ago. A group of drug dealers were growing dozens of small marijuana gardens alongside trickling streams in the LaSals far from the trails the hikers used. Their theory was that if one garden was discovered, the whole crop wouldn't be compromised. He smiled at the memory. It was during this case that he'd met Amy Rousseau.

So marijuana was a distinct possibility. If they were growing their own, there'd be no need for a supplier. Perhaps they grew the stuff and, being good citizens of the community, sold it to the villagers at an affordable price. Then what happened? Did something go wrong causing Sanchez to kill his buddies? Or had someone else set out to kill all three of them? And if so, what was the motive for the killings?

He shook his head. The problem with this theory was that it suffered from the same flaw as the owl poaching theory. If they were growing marijuana in the mountains, why go all the way to the LaSal Mountains in Utah to do it? Why not grow it right here in the Tusas Mountains? So the same old question still hung there—what was Archuleta doing in the LaSals?

He retrieved a beer from the refrigerator, popped it open, and took a swig. He wondered if the people of Santa Elena would be willing to discuss drugs with him if he raised the subject. Probably not, especially if they were users. Señor Abelardo Herrera, chief of the *cofradía,* had been the only one who had opened up. Perhaps Rivera should pay him another visit and broach the subject—see if he could make any headway. That thought caused Rivera to reflect on their conversation about the Penitentes, the *morada,* and the upcoming procession on Good Friday. Then he remembered what Herrera had said about the old *morada* and the girl who had committed suicide there. When did that happen?

With his iPhone, he searched on the words "santa elena, new mexico, suicide." That produced a number of references including an article which had appeared in the *Rio Grande Sun,* a weekly newspaper published in Española. Rivera was familiar with the publication. He'd seen a documentary on public television last year called *The Sun Never Sets* which described the history of the newspaper and how it had become nationally famous for its investigative journalism. Over the years, its journalists had exposed all kinds of wrongdoing and lawbreaking by public officials and wealthy businessmen in Rio Arriba County. As a result, a large collection of rocks was displayed prominently in the *Sun's* office. Each had been hurled through the newspaper's plate glass window by someone whose crooked deeds had been brought to light by the *Sun's* journalists. The newspaper staff had come to view the rocks as badges of honor.

Rivera read the article about the suicide. The girl's name was Angie Pacheco. She was 17 years old at the time of her death and lived in Canjilon. The article quoted the sheriff as saying she'd taken her life by leaping into Estaca Canyon. Since the bottom of the canyon was part of a popular hiking trail, a group of hikers from Arizona had discovered her body about an hour before dusk. They notified the authorities immediately. The sheriff went to the scene with a deputy and the Medical Examiner. The ME pronounced her dead and estimated the time of death at between noon and 1:00 P.M. The sheriff, after inspecting the area, proclaimed it to be a suicide.

Then Rivera looked at the date of the suicide. He was startled to learn it had taken place just a couple of days before David Archuleta was murdered in Utah.

19

THE AIR WAS cool and the morning sky clear as Rivera drove through the forest on his way to Santa Elena. He was alone again since Deputy Sheriff Gloria Valdez would be tied up in court awaiting her turn to testify as the arresting officer in an assault case. He'd discovered another voodoo figure attached to his vehicle this morning. This one looked like the first, except that two nails were penetrating its midsection instead of one. He'd tossed it into the vehicle's center console with its brother. He assumed this one carried the same sentiment as the first.

As he drove, he considered the possibility that Angie Pacheco's suicide was related to the Archuleta and Baeza shootings. There was no obvious reason to believe there was a connection, but the location of the suicide and its timing made it plausible and therefore deserving of further inquiry. Now he wanted to take a look at the place where it had happened.

He passed through Santa Elena and continued on the road to Estaca Canyon that Abelardo Herrera had pointed out to him. The road was a little-used two track grown over with weeds that wound its way through the pine trees. About a mile beyond the village, he came around a bend in the road and saw the old *morada* in a small clearing up ahead. A dusty GMC pickup truck was parked nearby.

Rivera parked next to the pickup and got out of his vehicle. The old *morada* was a small building constructed with adobe bricks and plastered with stucco. Much of the stucco had fallen off, exposing the bricks which were now weathering away. Without the stucco protection, each rainfall would remove a few more grains of soil from the bricks. Enough rain and the building would eventually collapse and dissolve back into the earth.

The entrance to the *morada* was a plank door. There was a single glass window, now yellowed with age, on each side of the structure. The roof was corrugated tin and a single cross was mounted above the door. Standing on a ridge behind the *morada* was a large cross constructed of pine beams stained dark brown.

Except for the birds chirping in the trees, the site had a profound silence. The view of Estaca Canyon from the *morada* was breathtaking. The terrain sloped down about thirty yards to the edge of a bluff, then dropped three hundred feet into the wide canyon below. Rivera walked to the edge of the bluff and peered into the canyon. It was populated with scrub oaks and wildflowers, and a clear creek gurgled through rocks and boulders which lay scattered in the bottom. Downstream, a small herd of elk grazed in the lush grass. The wall on the far side of the canyon was layered with yellow, orange, and purple strata. Beyond that, the terrain sloped upward into a pine forest. This beautiful spot was the place Angie Pacheco had chosen to end her life.

Rivera strolled back to the *morada* just as Flaco Chavez appeared from behind the building. He was raking the yard around the *morada*, a look of serene peace on his face, while humming a melody Rivera didn't recognize. He seemed totally absorbed in what he was doing and oblivious to Rivera's presence.

"Señor Chavez, may I have a word with you?"

Chavez kept working, not looking at Rivera, and not responding.

Rivera spoke louder. "Flaco?"

Chavez stopped raking and looked up. "*Sí*?"

Rivera switched to Spanish. "Do you remember me? We met yesterday."

"Yes."

He was a man of few words and apparently hard of hearing. Rivera wanted to ask him if he knew anything about the suicide, but he was concerned Flaco might clam up like most of the residents of Santa Elena. Rivera started with some non-threatening, general conversation. "Señor Herrera told me you've been raking the *morada* yards for forty years."

He smiled and seemed interested. "Yes. That's correct. It's because of a promise I made."

"A promise? To the Penitentes?"

"No, to God. I did something very bad in my youth. Very bad." His face took on a look of anguish. "This is my self-imposed penance. I promised God if he would forgive me, I'd keep the *morada* yard looking beautiful for the rest of my life."

"It looks like you do a very thorough job."

"Every morning, I get up, eat breakfast with my wife, and head out with my rake. It was hard at first—I don't mean physically. I mean it was just a nuisance I had to put up with each day. I became sorry I'd made the promise, but I kept it up. A promise is a promise." Chavez seemed to welcome the opportunity to tell his story. "Funny thing happened though. As the years went by, I began to take pleasure in it. It gave me purpose, and the people of Santa Elena began thanking me for my dedication to the beauty of our village. I felt needed by the community. And maybe by the good Lord too. I pictured him looking down each morning, hoping Flaco would get to work and make the *morada* yard look beautiful. When the new *morada* was built, I wasn't sure what he wanted me to do—keep raking the old yard or start raking the new one—so I decided I'd better do both."

Rivera smiled. "So now you enjoy doing it."

Chavez grinned and resumed raking. "Yes. Now it's what I look forward to each morning when I wake up. I'd miss it if I was unable to do it. Some people in the community like to kid me. They say that because I've grown to enjoy it, it's not really penance anymore."

Rivera laughed. "You've raked this yard every day for the past forty years?"

"Every day except the times I was too sick to get out of bed."

"Were you here the day that young girl from Canjilon committed suicide?"

He stopped raking and looked toward the canyon. "Yes, I was. I saw her standing down there by the cliff, looking into the canyon. She was still there when I left. I remember I was a little unhappy that day. I wanted to go into the *morada* to see what those young men were doing in there but they wouldn't allow me to enter. They had a key to the door and I didn't."

Rivera sucked in a breath and tried not to appear too anxious. "Some young men were in the *morada*? Who were they?"

There were three of them. After the new *morada* was built, they used this one as a meeting place. Let's see, it was Juan Baeza, David Archuleta, and Victor Sanchez. I didn't like that they used it but David was a Penitente like me, so there wasn't much I could say. But I always thought it was a little disrespectful that they treated the place like it was some kind of clubhouse."

"They were here the day Angie Pacheco committed suicide?"

"Yes."

"What were they doing?"

He shrugged. "I don't know. They met here every few days. I never could figure out what they were doing in there. I tried to go inside several times to see what was going on, but they always told me it was a private meeting. They wouldn't let me in. Maybe they thought I was too old to be their friend."

"Did you tell that to the sheriff?"

"There was no reason to. The sheriff said the girl's death was a suicide. Besides, that sheriff was a skunk. I was afraid of him. So was everyone else in the village."

"So when you left, the young men were still inside the old *morada* and Angie was still alive?"

"That's right." Flaco tossed the rake in the bed of his pickup. "I've got to go now. The yard at the new *morada* needs raking." He smiled. "Can't keep the good Lord waiting." He hopped into his vehicle and slowly drove off.

Rivera walked to the old *morada* and circled it, noting nothing unusual. He went to the front door and pushed on it. It was locked but he noticed the adobe around the wooden door jamb had weathered badly and the jamb itself was rotting. He pushed the jamb timber away from the door latch. The wood made a crunching sound as it compressed, and he was able to pull the door open. He shut his eyes and stepped back as a curtain of dust fell from above. He waited until it drifted away, wondering if what he was doing would be considered sacrilegious by the brothers of the *cofradía.* He glanced back down the road, scanned the area, and saw no one.

He peered into the *morada,* then stepped inside with care, ready to jump out if it began to collapse. Near a corner of the roof, some adobe bricks had weathered away completely and left a hole in the wall. The hole had allowed leaves and pine needles to accumulate inside the structure and cover the floor. It also allowed a shaft of sunlight to illuminate the interior. The room was empty except for three wooden chairs and a homemade table. Resting on the table was a cutting board. There were also a few items scattered on the floor—an old balance scale, a few rusted cutting knives, and a box of Ziploc bags similar to the ones Archuleta had been carrying in his backpack.

Now it looked even more like the three friends had been in the drug business—growing marijuana plants on federal land in the mountains, harvesting the buds as they became ripe, and transporting them out of the mountains in backpacks. He imagined them sitting here, packaging the buds in the plastic bags, and weighing the product on the scale. He wasn't sure about the purpose of the knives and the cutting board. Perhaps they were used to trim the stems off the buds.

He took photographs of the interior and close-ups of the paraphernalia on the table and floor. He stepped outside, closed the door, and returned the doorjamb to its original shape as best he could. He dusted himself off and walked to his vehicle. Rivera now had a little more information to work with. The picture of what had happened back then was by no means complete, but a few more pieces of the puzzle had fallen into place.

The crack of the gunshot from the woods on his left broke his train of thought as the dirt a few feet in front of him erupted in a cloud of dust. Reflexes kicked in—he crouched and sprinted, took cover behind his vehicle, and drew his Glock 19. He knelt on the ground, angry and fearful at the same time, trying to catch his breath. His heart was pounding.

He listened and heard nothing. The gunshot had frightened the birds into silence. He considered raising his head in an attempt to spot his assailant, but quickly rejected that idea. The shooter might be waiting for him to do exactly that. He knew Rivera's position, but Rivera only had a general idea of where the gunshot had come from. The sound was a rifle shot—there was no doubt in Rivera's mind about that. And the shooter was upslope from him, on the wooded hill that rose behind the *morada*. He judged the shooter was about forty yards away. Beyond that, the woods would be too thick for a clear shot. At that distance, his Glock would be no match for a rifle. Maybe there really was something to that *mal ojo* business. And maybe he should have taken the Sheriff's advice about not coming up here alone.

Rivera couldn't crouch behind his vehicle all day. He considered the gunshot—it was low and had missed him by about four feet. That struck him as odd. People living up here hunted game in the forest for food. They knew how to shoot. At forty yards, an experienced hunter with a rifle would have no trouble hitting a man square in the chest. He wouldn't have missed.

It was a warning shot, Rivera finally concluded, designed to scare him off. The logic was sound. Rivera figured it was safe to stand up, get in his vehicle, and just drive off. Still, would he want to bet his life on the correctness of that logic? Certainly not.

He reached up and opened the door to his vehicle. His pickup was equipped with a remote-control key fob. He reached into the vehicle, keeping his head down, and depressed the starter button. The engine roared to life. He waited for a gunshot and a bullet to tear through his windshield. None came.

As long as he kept the vehicle between him and the shooter, he'd be safe. He hoisted himself onto the running board. With one hand, he depressed the brake pedal and with the other, he slipped the gear-shift lever into reverse, feeling a slight lurch as the pickup began slowly backing down the road. Still no gunshot. He held the steering wheel with one hand, craned his neck so he could see the road, and guided the vehicle while hanging on the side like an outrigger. He struggled to keep it centered on the road, but from this unfamiliar viewpoint, that was nearly impossible. The pickup weaved from one side of the road to the other and back again.

He drove hanging in that position for a quarter mile. Soon, he spotted an old woman and a small boy picking berries in the woods next to the road. She watched him go by with a look of astonishment on her face. The boy was pointing, jumping up and down, and laughing with delight.

Figuring he was safe now, Rivera applied the brake and stopped. He climbed into the cab, made a U-turn, and drove back through Santa Elena and out of the mountains. He shook his head and wished the woman and boy hadn't seen him. That embarrassing story would be told to every resident of Santa Elena before sunset. It would probably become a part of the village's folklore for generations to come. Now he just wanted to get out of there without further loss of dignity.

20

RIVERA WAS NO stranger to gunfire—he'd found himself in some tight spots before. Only once had a bullet struck him. It had happened during a shootout in the backcountry with members of a drug running gang. Fortunately, it had been only a superficial flesh wound, tearing the skin on his arm and producing a lot of blood, but doing no damage to bone or muscle. The wound had stung for days. He'd never told anyone in his family about it—his mother had the idea that, as a deputy in rural Grand County, he was relatively safe from the perils of law enforcement that existed in the big cities. Rivera knew she worried about him anyway, but he wanted to spare her the added burden of worrying about bullets flying in the vicinity of her son.

On the drive back to Tierra Amarilla, his mind churned through the possibilities of who might have taken a shot at him. The exercise had produced no sensible answer. It did, however, raise another question. Who knew he would be at the old *morada* at that moment in time? Whoever fired the shot had to know in advance he was going to be there.

Flaco Chavez might have told someone after he'd returned to Santa Elena—but there hadn't been enough time for that person to grab a rifle, walk over a mile through the woods, and get in position to take the shot.

The only person he'd told of his plans to visit the old *morada* was Gloria Valdez. Might she have mentioned it to someone?

As he thought about the errant rifle shot, he became more convinced that it was only a warning—a shot designed to scare him off—just like the witch's *mal ojo*, the voodoo dolls, and the symbol drawn on the door of his motel room. Someone was trying to send him back to Utah with his tail between his legs.

In that sense, it was a good sign. It meant he was getting closer to the truth about David Archuleta's murder. His investigation was on the right track and someone was getting nervous about his probing. But Rivera realized he needed to be more careful. The tactics were escalating and a warning shot could be a precursor to something worse.

Setting the warnings aside, he now had a few more facts. First of all, the former sheriff had been beyond lax in his investigation of Angie Pacheco's suicide. It was common knowledge that Flaco was at the old *morada* every day. So why hadn't the sheriff questioned him? Clearly there had been no investigation at all, so it was entirely possible her death had not been a suicide. If she had been deliberately killed, could the former sheriff himself have been involved? Had he agreed to look the other way as a favor to someone? Rio Arriba County had a reputation for corruption, so that possibility couldn't be ruled out.

Rivera had learned some interesting new facts about David Archuleta and his two buddies. They were at the old *morada* on a regular basis. If they were, in fact, growing marijuana on public lands and packaging it at the old *morada*, might Angie have learned what they were doing the day she was there? Perhaps she'd stood outside the old *morada* and heard some of their conversation. Could they have shoved her over the cliff to protect the secrecy of their little business?

And that thought suggested another possible scenario. If Archuleta and his buddies had killed her, perhaps someone had learned what they'd done and set out to exact revenge. And maybe Victor Sanchez had deduced that possibility after Archuleta disappeared and Baeza was shot, so he left town. Rivera considered that thesis. It didn't seem consistent with the character of the young men, but it couldn't be ruled out.

There was also the possibility that Sanchez had killed his two partners over some disagreement about how to spend or split the profits from the marijuana operation—but that theory suffered from the same problem. Committing murder didn't seem consistent with what he'd learned about Sanchez's character. Nevertheless, it too couldn't be ruled out.

Rivera shook his head. There were too many possibilities. And there was still the key question he'd been unable to answer all along. Why would Archuleta grow marijuana in the LaSals when he could just as easily have grown it in the mountains around Santa Elena? None of this was making any sense.

He was pondering his next move when his iPhone rang. It was Amy.

"Hi, handsome. I'm lonely. When are you coming back to Moab?"

"I don't know. This investigation is getting more and more involved. I think I'll be here awhile." He summarized what he'd learned since coming to Rio Arriba County but omitted any mention of the gunshot.

"It sounds like you're making progress. Have you thought any more about moving to Albuquerque?"

"Honestly, Amy, I've been so busy that I haven't had time to think it through. But I promise we'll talk about it as soon as I get back to Moab."

"Fair enough. Anyway, the reason I called was to tell you what my scientist friends were able to deduce from the drawings in Archuleta's journal."

Rivera perked up. "Did they find anything useful?"

"We're scientists, Manny. We're in search of new knowledge. We don't worry about whether it's useful or not. Have you forgotten everything I've taught you?"

He laughed. It was fun to banter with Amy again, even if it was only on the phone. He missed her. "Okay, what did you geniuses come up with?"

"Well, to be honest, not a whole lot. According to our animal biologist, the animals depicted in the drawings are all indigenous to the Four Corners states. Nothing unusual there. Our botanist, that would be me, concluded pretty much the same thing about the trees, bushes, and flowers Archuleta had drawn in the journal. They were species you'd expect to find in Utah, Colorado, New Mexico, and even west Texas. Our resident lichenologist was unable to conclude anything about the drawings of the lichen-covered rocks, except that they probably existed at altitudes over four thousand feet. Our two geologists looked at the drawings of the rock formations. Southwest United States was all they could deduce. One of them, an older professor from Stanford, noticed the drawings of the mushrooms. He's not a mycologist, but he said he recognized a couple of them from his days in college."

"What's a mycologist?"

"Someone who studies fungi. Anyway, he said they were psilocybin mushrooms. He and his college buddies at Berkeley used to search for them in the Sierra Madre Mountains during spring break. He said back in those days, he spent a lot of time hanging out with hippies and itinerant musicians in Haight-Ashbury, the epicenter of the drug counter-culture."

"Sillo-what?"

"Psilocybin. You know, psychedelic mushrooms. The hallucinogenic type more commonly known as magic mushrooms or 'shrooms."

"Of course. 'Shrooms would make more sense than marijuana," said Rivera, almost to himself. "Thanks, Amy. That's helpful. I've got to run. I'm just pulling up in front of the sheriff's office right now."

He parked alongside the curb and sat there, thinking. Psychedelic mushrooms fit the clues better than marijuana. If Archuleta and his buddies were selling marijuana, they wouldn't have needed the knives and cutting board he'd seen in the old *morada*. They would have picked the ripe buds off the cannabis plants and left the stems in place. They would have packaged the buds directly without the need of knives and a cutting board. With mushrooms, slicing them would allow tighter packaging in the Ziploc bags. Archuleta had been in the LaSals collecting psychedelic mushrooms.

His excitement at this new revelation ended as quickly as it had started when he realized the mushroom theory suffered from the same problem as the marijuana theory. Why collect mushrooms in the LaSals when you could do the same thing locally in the Tusas Mountains?

21

RIVERA SPOTTED GLORIA Valdez walking toward the sheriff's building. He lowered the window of his vehicle and called out to her. She walked over with a smile. Tilted her head. "Hi," she said softly. "I've missed our mountain adventures together."

He knew what she wanted him to say—that he missed her too. She was a beauty and he was attracted to her, but his life was already complicated enough. He smiled. "You're missing all the fun. How are things going in court?"

"We're recessed for lunch. I'm due back in an hour. I haven't been called to testify yet. The lawyers are arguing about whether some testimony from a previous trial is admissible in this trial. Meanwhile, I twiddle my thumbs and wait."

Rivera got out of his pickup. "I learned something interesting today."

"What's that?"

"Do you remember hearing about a young girl who committed suicide by jumping off a bluff into Estaca Canyon?"

"It sounds vaguely familiar."

"It happened fifteen years ago. Her name was Angie Pacheco. It turns out she jumped just a couple of days before David Archuleta was killed."

"You think there's a connection?"

"Maybe. Here's the interesting part. She jumped at a place about thirty yards downslope from the old *morada* near Santa Elena. The *morada* was abandoned after the Penitentes built the new one in the village. Archuleta, Baeza, and Sanchez were inside the old *morada* the day she jumped."

Gloria's eyebrows went up. "Really? How did you learn that?"

"I talked to a man named Flaco Chavez. He rakes the area around both *moradas* every day. It's a form of penance he does. He said the three of them were there that day. When he left, Angie was still alive and the three young men were still inside the old *morada*."

She nodded her head as she digested the implications. "That is *very* interesting."

"I'd like to take a look at the file on the Pacheco suicide," said Rivera.

"Sure. Let's go inside and I'll get it for you."

"Wait. Before we go in there, I need to ask you a question. Did you mention to anyone that I was going to visit the old *morada* today?"

She thought for a moment. “I told the sheriff.”

“Did anyone overhear you?”

“The sheriff was standing in front of my desk when I told him. Ruby and Gilbert Jaramillo were in the area. Why?”

“Someone fired a shot at me as I was leaving the old *morada*.”

Her face paled. “No kidding. You okay?”

“I’m fine. Whoever it was had to know I was going there. Jaramillo eavesdrops on our discussions—then afterwards, when we’re finished, he always returns to his desk and makes a telephone call. I think he’s been reporting everything we say to someone outside the department.”

“That wouldn’t surprise me. There aren’t many secrets in Rio Arriba County. Did you see who fired the shot?”

“No. It came from somewhere in the forest. The bullet missed me by a wide margin so I think it was just a warning. Someone wants me to leave town.”

“I don’t know what to say. Maybe you should wait until I’m out of court before you go back there. It would be a lot safer with backup.”

He nodded. “Probably right. Let’s go inside and take a look at that Pacheco file.”

Rivera was relieved to see that Gilbert Jaramillo was out to lunch. At least there would be a modicum of privacy. He sat in a chair next to Gloria’s desk and thumbed through the Pacheco file. Angie Pacheco lived in the village of Canjilon. She was seventeen years old and had just graduated from high school near the top of her class. The file contained a photograph of her that looked like a graduation picture. She was dark eyed and pretty with long hair. She was flashing a beautiful smile, the kind that would draw smiles from anyone who saw it. There were several other photos of her in the file which were taken at the bottom of Estaca Canyon. In these, she wasn't pretty.

A group of hikers from Arizona who were on a trail through the canyon had discovered her body about 5:00 P.M. The Medical Examiner estimated the time of death at between noon and 1:00 P.M.

Two pieces of information in the file jumped out at Rivera. First, the former sheriff had investigated the matter. In a half page report, he simply declared the death was a suicide. There was no investigation at all; it was more like an offhand opinion. Rivera couldn't believe a law officer would be so derelict in his duties. The man was right where he belonged—in prison. The second thing that caught Rivera's attention was in the Medical Examiner's report. Angie was ten weeks pregnant when she died.

He looked at Gloria. "I'm going to Canjilon this afternoon. I want to talk to the Pacheco family."

"What about?"

"I'm not sure. I just want to find out more about Angie. Maybe she had some connection with Archuleta and his two friends."

"Why don't you wait until I'm out of court? Maybe I should go with you."

Rivera looked at his watch. "I'll be alright."

"Well, okay. Be careful up there."

Rivera drove to Canjilon, still feeling a discomfort in his stomach. Rather than fading with time, it seemed to be getting worse. It wasn't the typical gastro-intestinal pain one gets after a night of excessive eating and drinking. It was nothing like he'd experienced before.

At the edge of town, he came upon three men repairing a small house made of adobe bricks. Each was clad in the uniform typical of craftsmen who work outdoors—a straw hat, a sweat-stained long-sleeve shirt, jeans, and work boots. He pulled his vehicle off to the side of the road and stopped. The walls of the house had weathered badly and one of them had partially collapsed. It appeared the structure had been abandoned for many years and was now being made ready for reuse.

An old, dusty pickup was parked in front of the house, its bed filled with tools and sacks of material. A portable CD player with the volume turned up sat on the hood of the vehicle. Rivera smiled when he heard the sound of mariachis singing *Viva El Amor.* One of the men, who was slathering stucco cement over the adobe bricks, sang along in a loud, passionate voice. It was the song Rivera's father used to sing to his mother when he was in a playful mood.

He'd drop down on one knee, throw out his arms, and belt it out while his mother grinned from ear to ear and the kids laughed at the spectacle. Whenever his father sang that song to his mother, it made the whole family happy.

Rivera got out of his pickup and watched one of the other men work. With his trowel, he expertly laid down a bed of cement exactly the right shape, placed an adobe brick on top of it, tapped on the brick with the handle of his trowel, scraped off the excess cement, and repeated the process with precision and seemingly without effort. The third man noticed Rivera standing there and walked over to him. His clothing was covered with dust and cement and his hands were caked with stucco. Rivera had become a little more proficient at talking to these people—he knew better than to ask him directly where the Pacheco family lived.

He spoke in Spanish, telling the man about how his father loved to sing that song to his mother, and how the kids got a big kick out of it. They laughed and chatted about that for a while. Then they talked about mariachis and which songs were their favorite *corridos*. Then the man said they didn't get many Utah policemen in Canjilon. Rivera told him he was here to visit the Pacheco residence.

"Which Pacheco? Pedro Pacheco, Rosa Pacheco, Hilario Pacheco, or Luisa Pacheco Flores?"

"I'm not sure." Rivera decided he'd better come clean. "I want to talk to the family of Angie Pacheco, the girl who committed suicide at Estaca Canyon fifteen years ago."

"Her parents are deceased. You want to talk to her sister. That would be Luisa." He told Rivera how to find her house. By now the other two men had joined them and stood there smiling and nodding.

"Thanks very much," said Rivera. He turned to leave.

One of the other men spoke up. "Hey, Señor. We heard about a stunt driver from Utah. He can drive his pickup backwards while hanging out the door on the running board. Do you know him?"

The other men grinned.

Rivera laughed. "You know, it's amazing how quickly you can learn how to drive like that when someone is shooting at you."

Their smiles faded. The men withdrew, told him to be careful, and went back to work.

As Rivera drove, he had to grin. The story of his stunt driving had spread from one mountain village to another in a matter of only a few hours. Already, he'd achieved fame in Rio Arriba County.

He found the residence of Luisa Pacheco Flores, Angie's sister, and knocked on the door. When Luisa opened it, Rivera could see the striking family resemblance between her and the photo of Angie in the case file. He apologized for the intrusion, told her he was investigating an old Utah murder case, and asked for a few minutes of her time. She spoke to him in the doorway rather than inviting him inside.

"The baby is sleeping," she explained.

"Did you know a man by the name of David Archuleta?"

She thought for a moment, shook her head. "No."

"How about Juan Baeza or Victor Sanchez?"

"I've heard of Juan Baeza. He was killed in a hunting accident a long time ago. I think he was some kind of football star."

"They all lived in Santa Elena. I think they might have seen your sister the day she committed suicide. I wanted to find out if there was a connection between Angie and one of those men."

Luisa became visibly upset. She stepped outside and closed the door. "The sheriff said Angie committed suicide but I never believed it." Her eyes began to tear up. "Angie was smart and pretty and popular. She had no reason to end her life. Absolutely none."

"Did you know she was pregnant when she died?"

Luisa lowered her head. "Yes, I knew. Angie wasn't married and I was her older sister, so she confided in me. We talked a lot about what she should do. She said she wanted to have the baby whether or not the father would marry her. She was happy about being pregnant and couldn't wait to become a mother."

"Did she say who the father was?"

"No, she wouldn't tell me. But I think he might have lived in Santa Elena."

"Did she say whether the father planned to marry her?"

"She said he needed some time to think about it."

"She was underage," said Rivera. "Maybe she didn't want to get the father in trouble with the law."

Luisa smiled. "Señor, around here, some girls have babies at fifteen."

"That bluff where she died is a long way from Canjilon. Do you know how Angie got there that day?"

"The morning of the day she died, she asked me to drive her to Santa Elena. She said she'd arranged to meet with the baby's father at noon. That's what made me think he lived in Santa Elena."

"You didn't drive her all the way to the bluff?"

"No. She said she wanted to walk the last mile. I dropped her off in the village about eleven o'clock and came back home."

22

AFTER A CHEESEBURGER at Pete's Deluxe Dining Room that evening, Rivera drove back to the motel. The sun had set and daylight was fading. The outside temperature was dropping fast and a brisk breeze descended from the mountains as the high-altitude air cooled and became heavier. He held onto his hat and trotted from his vehicle to his room. As he reached for the doorknob, he saw another voodoo doll hanging from it by a length of string. It looked like the other two, only this one had three nails stuck through the midsection.

The mild queasiness in his stomach had persisted since he'd been the recipient of the *mal ojo* in Santa Elena. If there was anything at all to this witchcraft business, Rivera figured, the effects of the *mal ojo* would certainly be amplified by the voodoo figures with nails driven through their stomachs. As soon as he had those thoughts, he shook his head and rejected them. There was no such thing as witchcraft.

He sat down at the small desk in his room and considered the current state of his investigation. He was acquiring more and more information, but still had no idea what Archuleta was doing in the LaSals. He took out a pad and jotted down the key events in chronological order.

1. Archuleta, Baeza, and Sanchez in the psychedelic mushroom business.

2. Angie Pacheco, pregnant, commits suicide. Pushed? Flaco was there that day. So were Archuleta, Baeza, and Sanchez.

3. Archuleta shot in LaSals. No vehicle.

4. Baeza shot in Tusas Mtns. Same rifle.

5. Sanchez disappears (is still alive somewhere).

6. Former sheriff derelict in his duties. No investigation of Baeza or Pacheco deaths. Years later, he's found to be corrupt.

Rivera studied the sequence. What were the possible motives that might tie all of these events together? Rivera's gut instinct told him the events on the list had to be linked in some way. He searched his mind but was unable to zero in on a sensible idea. Sheriff Bradshaw had always taught him to step back from the details and take a larger view, but, as yet, Rivera was unable to see the big picture.

His iPhone rang. It was Millie Ives, his dispatcher, calling from Moab.

"How are you doing in New Mexico?"

"Hi, Millie. I guess I'm making some progress but I haven't identified our killer yet. How are things going with this year's Jeep Safari?"

"Oh, same as usual. A couple of rollovers and a few medical emergencies. Very manageable so far."

"I'm glad to hear that." Rivera knew there had to be an important point to this call. It wasn't often he received a call from his dispatcher while she was off duty. He waited.

"Manny, I'm calling you from home. This call is unofficial. Sheriff Campbell has asked me a couple of times if you've checked in. When I told him no, he seemed irritated."

"Yeah, I should have reported in. I've been so busy, I just forgot."

"He said maybe you're taking a vacation on the county dime and having too much fun to bother with a call. I think he was trying to be funny but no one in the office seems to appreciate his sense of humor."

"He's angry with me more than usual. He thinks I'm going to run for sheriff."

"Oh, what a good idea." She laughed. "But don't quote me on that."

"I let him think I was running even though I have no intention of getting into the race. I don't think I'd enjoy the job. I like what I'm doing now."

"Why is he always so mad at you? I mean, he's rude to everybody, but it seems he's especially so with you."

"He thinks I enforce some of the laws and ignore others. And I do, when I think it's the right thing to do."

"Well, sure. Sheriff Bradshaw was the same way. You have to use some judgment. But he seems to go overboard with you. There must be more to it than that."

Rivera hesitated. He'd never repeated what his friend Emmett Mitchell had once told him about Denny Campbell when Campbell had first become sheriff. But Millie was a friend and confidant. She'd been working in the Sheriff's Office for three decades as a dispatcher, so she was more like a den mother to the deputies and, Rivera knew, she was particularly fond of him. They had developed a close camaraderie in the five years he'd worked there.

"Millie, can I tell you something about Sheriff Campbell that has to remain just between the two of us?"

"Of course, Manny. I won't repeat it."

"Sheriff Campbell sees himself as a real macho man. At least he acts that way. Truth is, I think he's very insecure. A few years ago, right after he moved to Moab, his wife ran off with a younger man to a California commune. She'd made it known to friends that she'd had enough of him and needed a new life where she could find love and happiness. Campbell was furious. He went to the commune intending to bring her back but she refused to come with him. He pleaded with her but her mind was made up—she wouldn't budge. What made it worse was that she and her boyfriend and the others in the commune all laughed at Campbell as he was leaving. It must have been terribly humiliating for him. Since then, he's been tough on everyone."

"That's sad but it's still no reason to treat you the way he does."

"The man she ran off with was Hispanic. I learned later he looked a lot like me."

"Oh, my. That might explain it."

"Knowing his history helps me put up with his rudeness—he's torn up inside. But one day, I may decide I've had enough of him and move on."

"I hope that day never comes. Anyway, I just thought I'd let you know he was asking about you."

"Thanks, Millie. I'll try to check in more often. I appreciate the call."

Just as soon as he clicked off, his phone buzzed again.

"Manny, it's Leroy Bradshaw. I think we may have located your man."

"That's good news. I've reached a point where I'm kind of stuck."

"Those phone calls to the Sanchez residence in Santa Elena came from a man named Victor Suarez. He lives in Santa Fe."

"I guess Sanchez is going by the name Suarez now. He doesn't want to be found, so a name change would be logical."

"He lives in an apartment on Cerrillos Road and does income tax returns for a living. He doesn't have an office—works out of his apartment. Apparently he lives alone." Bradshaw read off the address.

"I'm going down there in the morning," said Rivera. "I need to pay him a visit and find out a few things."

"You'd better be careful. If he's the one who killed his two friends, you might be walking into a bad situation."

"I know. Trouble is, I can't count on Sheriff Gallegos for any help. It's outside of his jurisdiction. And I don't want to get local law enforcement involved."

"Why not?"

"If Sanchez is an innocent man and left Santa Elena because he feared for his life, I don't want to expose him to the killer by revealing his whereabouts."

"Makes sense. But still, you shouldn't go there alone. Look, I'm right here in Santa Fe. I'll go with you. It'll be like old times."

"But Sheriff, you've got a business to run."

"Where and when do we meet? And Manny, it's okay to call me Leroy."

23

LEROY BRADSHAW'S OFFICE was located on the second floor of a three-story brick building in an office park just outside of downtown Santa Fe. Rivera entered the spacious lobby and walked up a flight of stairs. He found a polished wood door with *Bradshaw Investigations LLC* inscribed on it in gold lettering. He entered and was greeted by a cheerful, attractive woman in her fifties whose dress, diction, and manner projected a quiet competence.

"Welcome, Deputy Rivera. I'm Patricia, Mr. Bradshaw's administrative assistant." She extended her hand and gave him a firm handshake. "Mr. Bradshaw will want to see you right away. Please follow me."

Rivera wondered how she knew who he was. He was out of uniform, wearing Wrangler jeans and a yellow dress shirt. A lightweight, blue blazer concealed his shoulder holster and handgun. Bradshaw must have given her a pretty good description.

She led him through a plush clerical area and down a hallway past a half dozen offices with heavy, dark doors. He glanced into the offices with open doors as he passed them, seeing a young man with a goatee and an intense expression staring at a monitor and typing on his keyboard, an older woman with stylish glasses poring over a thick document, and a beefy man in his forties wearing a white shirt with his sleeves rolled up, gesturing while he talked on the phone.

Rivera couldn't get the *Mr. Bradshaw* out of his head. Didn't she know he was Sheriff Bradshaw?

She knocked lightly on the door at the end of the hallway.

"Come in," said a familiar voice.

She opened the door with a smile and gestured Rivera into the office. Leroy Bradshaw looked up from the papers on his desk and grinned. He came around his large mahogany desk and gave Rivera a bear hug. "It's so good to see you, Manny."

They sat in overstuffed leather chairs by the window. "Thanks for helping me out today," said Rivera. "Until you volunteered to come along, I wasn't really sure how I was going to handle the Sanchez visit."

"From what you told me on the phone, it sounds like you're making good progress on the case."

"It's moving along but I still have a lot of unanswered questions. I'm hoping Sanchez can fill in some of the blanks." Rivera's eyes scanned the office as he spoke. He was struck with an intense feeling of nostalgia. The office looked a lot like Bradshaw's office in Moab when he was sheriff. On a table in the corner was the same coffee maker he'd had in Moab. And the framed photographs on the wall were the same—Moab's Main Street in the 1950s, the sheriff's department intramural softball team, and beautiful landscape scenes of Grand County. Rivera was in the softball team photo. Perhaps that explained how Bradshaw's administrative assistant recognized him. A few new photographs had been added to the collection—the Santa Fe Indian Market, the Loretto Chapel, and some landscape shots which captured Santa Fe at sunset nestled in the foothills of the Sangre de Cristo Mountains. On his desk was a photograph of Jill, his deceased wife.

Bradshaw looked good but he'd never regained the weight he'd lost after Jill had passed away. His blond hair was combed straight back just as Rivera remembered, but now it was a little thinner and traces of gray had appeared. The ever-inquisitive look in his piercing blue eyes was the same as it had been when he was sheriff of Grand County.

"It'll take about fifteen minutes to drive to Sanchez's apartment. You want some coffee before we head out?"

"Thanks, but I think I'll pass. My stomach is a little queasy today."

"You look a little pale. Everything okay?"

"I'm fine. It's nothing. Maybe something I ate." Rivera wasn't about to tell Bradshaw a witch had cast an evil spell on him.

"Did you drive down in your unit?"

"Yes."

"Then let's take my car. No sense advertising you're a deputy from Utah. If Sanchez is our killer, we don't want to give him any advanced warning."

"Good idea." Rivera noticed that Bradshaw had said *our killer.* He liked that. Bradshaw still saw the Archuleta murder as his case—an unmet responsibility that still hung over him—even after all these years.

Just outside his office, Bradshaw stopped in front of a closed door. "This is the office I've been saving for you." He opened the door.

Rivera looked inside. A large window had a clear view of the Sangre de Cristo Mountains and the furniture was dark wood instead of gray metal. "Pretty plush," said Rivera. "And a great view of the mountains."

"I remember how much you liked a mountain view."

They walked to the parking lot, got into Bradshaw's white Toyota Avalon, and headed for the Sanchez residence.

"So what do you think about coming to Santa Fe permanently?" asked Bradshaw.

"Amy received an offer to become an assistant professor at UNM in Albuquerque. She wants me to move down there. Working in Santa Fe might be a good option. I just don't know. I think I'd miss the red rock canyon country around Moab."

"Well, consider it. You can come to work for me anytime you want. I could probably give you a substantial salary increase."

"What kind of cases does your firm work on?"

"We work mostly for wealthy individuals and law firms. Some corporate stuff. The work usually involves documenting an individual's activities or tracking financial transactions."

Rivera nodded. That didn't sound very interesting to him. He remained silent.

"I know what you're thinking," said Bradshaw. "The work sounds boring and tedious—and it is at times, but sometimes it can be quite interesting. Even exciting."

Rivera decided to change the subject before Bradshaw made another attempt to recruit him. "When you first moved down here, you lived in Abiquiu, didn't you?"

"Yeah. That was a rough couple of months. I was down in the dumps after Jill's passing. I rented a house trailer in Abiquiu and just sat around all day doing nothing. I stayed in the trailer most of the time. I never met any of the locals—didn't really want to, I guess. I hit the bottle pretty hard during that time. I wore the same clothes every day and rarely shaved. I kept wondering why she'd been taken from me. She was the center of my life and when she died, I thought my life was over."

Rivera didn't know what to say. He knew Bradshaw had been crushed by his wife's death but Rivera could never have pictured his former boss alone in a rented trailer, depressed and drinking every day. "I'm glad you pulled through it okay. It looks like you have a good life now."

"It's better now but I still think about our time in Moab and wish I had all that back. Jill was an amazing woman. She did a lot of volunteer work around town. She tutored kids at the high school, helped in the kitchen at the Moab Home for Needy Children, and even volunteered to pick up trash along the highway. She wasn't the type to have titles and serve on boards—she preferred to get involved doing the work and interacting with those who needed help. In the evenings, we'd have dinner and talk about what we'd done during the day. I miss that."

"Ever think about coming back to Moab? We could use a good sheriff."

Bradshaw laughed. "I take it Denny Campbell hasn't mellowed. Is he still on your case?"

"Almost every day."

"So why don't *you* run for sheriff? His term will be up in a year or so."

"I prefer to do investigative work. It's what I enjoy the most."

"And you're very good at it. Truth is, I *have* thought about returning a time or two—but the business is going well and I'm slowly building a new life here. I do intend to come back to Moab for a visit sometime soon."

"Great. Everyone asks about you. We'll roll out the red carpet."

"You know what got me out of that trailer in Abiquiu? What got me moving again?"

"What?"

"It was that telephone call I got from you a couple of months after I left Moab."

"Really? I should have called sooner, I guess, but I figured you'd call the office when you got settled in. When we didn't hear from you, I decided to make the call."

Bradshaw turned onto Cerrillos Road. "Talking to you kind of woke me up. You said something about hanging in there—that all bad times eventually pass. You said there was a role for everyone in life, and that I just needed to find mine. You reminded me that I had good investigative skills that shouldn't go to waste—something like that. Anyway, it got me thinking more about the future and less about my problems." He laughed. "I shaved that day, dumped the Jim Beam down the drain, and started making plans to set up the new company."

24

"THERE IT IS on the right," said Rivera, pointing to a complex of eight Spanish style apartment buildings with tan walls and red tile roofs. A manager's office, tennis court, and clubhouse were located in front of the complex and covered parking spaces occupied the outer perimeter. There was a parking area for visitors next to the manager's office. Bradshaw slowed down and turned into the first driveway he came to.

"I'll drive around back and see if I can find an empty spot," said Bradshaw. "No sense attracting attention by waltzing through the front of the complex."

"Good idea. The fewer people that see us, the better."

The covered parking spaces were numbered and reserved for residents. Bradshaw found an uncovered space without a number next to a dumpster and pulled into it. They entered the complex from the rear and walked past a swimming pool, now unoccupied because of the chilly morning air.

They climbed a flight of stairs, located Unit 216, and knocked on the door. A man opened the door right away with a smile and a look of enthusiasm. When he saw his visitors, the smile disappeared.

"Oh. I was expecting someone else. Can I help you?"

Rivera spotted the jagged scar over the man's right eyebrow and knew instantly he was Victor Sanchez, despite the shorter hair and the beard he'd grown. He introduced himself and Bradshaw, and asked if they could have a word with him.

"What's this about?"

"It's better if we discuss it inside."

"I don't think so." He started to close the door.

"We know who you are, Victor Sanchez," said Rivera.

Sanchez hesitated. "You have the wrong address. My name is Suarez."

"I'm investigating the murder of your old friend David Archuleta and I need to ask you a few questions. In private. If you close that door, I'll have no choice but to come back here with local law enforcement. That'll mean exposure of your real identity, so if you want to continue living under your alias, you'll talk to us."

Sanchez's eyes shifted from Rivera to Bradshaw and back to Rivera. A sheen of perspiration appeared on his forehead, despite the cool temperature. "You don't know what you're doing. You could get me killed."

That remark told Rivera that Sanchez had fled Santa Elena out of fear for his own life, not because he'd killed his two friends. "Let us come inside, ask our questions, and leave. If we're satisfied with your answers, no one need know about any of this."

Sanchez pulled the door open and nodded for them to come in. He peered outside looking right and left before he closed the door.

He gestured toward a couch. "Now that you've ruined my day, have a seat."

The apartment was small and the furniture plain but comfortable. On a bookshelf were several framed photographs—one of his parents, one of his sister and Rosita, and another of Rosita and Perrito. The photos were recent, probably mailed to Sanchez by his father. There was a fourth photograph, larger than the others, which showed the village of Santa Elena. The photo was taken from a higher, distant vantage point, and captured the peaceful essence of the mountain village.

Rivera got right to the point. "My investigation concerns murder. I have no interest in dredging up information to build a case against three young men who were selling dope fifteen years ago."

Sanchez nodded. "It doesn't matter—the statute of limitations ran out on all that years ago. I know because I checked—I counted the days until I was safe. I'm a good citizen now and I don't want any trouble with the law."

"Well, let's start with the dope business. Can you run through the whole operation for me? How did that work?"

"I thought you said you weren't interested in that."

"I'm not interested in building a case on dope dealing but it's part of a larger picture I need to understand."

"Alright, I understand. Well, the three of us—me, David, and Juan Baeza—grew up in Santa Elena and were lifelong buddies. David was sort of our leader. He was admitted into the *cofradía* at an early age and therefore had achieved some measure of stature in the community. He was a serious and devout member of the Brotherhood. The Penitente beliefs and values had a profound influence on him and he wanted to devote his life to doing good things for the community. He persuaded Juan and me to join him in helping the people who couldn't help themselves.

"We needed money for supplies, tools, materials, and so forth. We repaired our neighbors' homes, fixed their equipment and machinery, and bought school supplies or food or whatever was necessary. So much work was needed in the community that we quickly ran out of our own money. The shortage of funds was limiting how much we could help the people and that frustrated David. One day, he told Juan and me he'd found a solution to the problem and asked us to join him in what he called a business venture. We were all best friends since the time we could walk, so we said yes. The business venture was collecting 'shrooms—you know, magic mushrooms—and selling them. David had learned all about them from a guy who'd moved to New Mexico from Colorado. They'd worked together part time for a while at the highway department. David passed on what he'd learned about mushrooms to Juan and me—where to find them, which ones were edible, which ones were poisonous, which ones were psychedelic—and from that day on we were in business. It was all profit because we hardly had any expenses. Our labor was free and the mushrooms grew right there in the forest. We weren't users ourselves—we sold everything we harvested."

"How did you market them?"

We'd slice them and package them in the abandoned *morada.* Every few days, we'd drive to Española, meet a guy from Albuquerque, and swap the 'shrooms for cash. We used all the money to help people in the community. Honestly, it's probably the one thing I've done in my life that I'm proudest of."

Rivera nodded. "Yeah, I can understand that." He thought for a moment. "David Archuleta had a box of Ziploc bags in his backpack, so I'm assuming he was in the LaSal Mountains to collect mushrooms. Is that right?"

"That's right."

"And that would explain why he had a backpack instead of a daypack. He needed the extra room for the mushrooms he was going to collect. But here's the thing I don't understand. Mushrooms grow everywhere. If you were able to collect them locally in the Tusas Mountains, why was Archuleta a couple of hundred miles away collecting them in the LaSal Mountains?

"Aha," said Bradshaw, slapping his knee. He'd been silent up to that point.

Rivera looked at him. "What?"

"I think I just figured out that part of the puzzle."

"Tell me."

"Rainfall," said Bradshaw.

"Exactly right," said Sanchez.

"What do you mean?" asked Rivera.

"We had a dry period for about a month in the Tusas Mountains," said Sanchez. "Mushrooms sprout after a wet spell so there was nothing to collect locally. But there had been a fair amount of rain up in Utah. We needed cash to buy some materials for a couple of projects we were working on, so we got in my pickup and headed to Utah. We stayed one night in Moab, then got up early the next morning and headed into the LaSals. I dropped David off at Haystack Mountain, Juan at Mount Mellenthin, and I took Mount Peale. The idea was for the three of us to collect 'shrooms all day. Then, around sunset, I'd pick up David and Juan in the same places I'd dropped them off and we'd head back home. It doesn't take long to gather a backpack full of product if you know what you're doing and where to look. At the end of the day, I picked up Juan and we headed for Haystack Mountain to get David. When we got close to the place where we'd dropped him off, we came upon a couple of sheriff's vehicles and an EMS unit. There was a small group of hikers nearby watching what was going on. From them, we learned that David had been shot and killed. They said that, according to the Medical Examiner, he'd been lying there all day. It must have happened shortly after we dropped him off. We panicked and got out of there. We dumped out the 'shrooms before leaving the mountains and headed back to Santa Elena. That was the end of our business."

"Any idea who shot him?'

"Juan and I talked about that all the way home. We were kind of devastated. David had been our buddy for as long as we could remember. He didn't have an enemy in the world. Everyone loved him. The only thing we could figure out was that the guy we were selling the 'shrooms to, or maybe one of his competitors, got mad at David for some reason."

"Then, a couple of days later, Juan was shot and killed," prompted Rivera.

"Right. That's when I figured someone was out to get all three of us. The sheriff we had back then claimed it was a hunting accident, but I knew better. I packed my bags and left. I came to Santa Fe, changed my name, grew a beard to change my appearance, and started a new life."

"Well, that answers a lot of my questions. Who was your buyer from Albuquerque?"

"David set it up so I'm sure he knew the guy's full name. I only knew him as Pancho."

"You never heard his last name?"

"No."

"Anything you can recall that might help us identify him?"

He shook his head. "Not really. He was in his thirties, I'd say, with long dark hair, a round face, and a big belly. Looked half Hispanic and half Anglo. Tattoos on his arms. He was kind of a sloppy looking guy. But that was fifteen years ago."

"A couple of days before David was killed, Angie Pacheco jumped off the cliff into Estaca Canyon. You and your two friends were at the old *morada* that day according to Flaco Chavez. Do you remember seeing Angie there?"

Sanchez sat back in his chair. Nodded. "Yeah, I saw her. We were inside the old *morada* and Flaco knocked on the door. He asked if he could join us. He often did that. Like always, I told him it was a private meeting and he couldn't come inside. We liked Flaco but we didn't want him to know what we were doing. He was quite a bit older than us and we didn't know how he'd react if he knew we were selling illegal drugs. Before closing the door, I glanced around outside and saw

Angie standing at the edge of the bluff. A few minutes later, we heard Flaco drive off in his pickup."

"Was anyone with Angie when you saw her?"

"No. She was standing there looking back down the road. I remember she glanced at her watch. I got the impression she was waiting for someone."

"Did she see you?"

"I don't think so."

"Was she still there when you left the *morada*?"

"No. At least I didn't see her."

"Did you see anyone else in the area when you left?"

He thought, shook his head. "No."

"Did the three of you leave the old *morada* together?"

"Yes."

"Do you remember what time that was?"

"Oh man, that was a long time ago. Let's see. I'd guess it was around noon or one o'clock because after we left, we went to David's house for lunch."

"Did you tell the sheriff any of this?"

"No way. I always tried to avoid that man. Remember, I was selling illegal drugs at the time. And besides, I didn't learn about Angie's death until Juan and I came back from Moab. By then, David had been killed and Juan and I were freaked out. A couple of days later, Juan was killed and I split."

"One last thing that has to do with some items David Archuleta carried in his backpack." Rivera told Sanchez about the owl feathers and the *La Santa Muerte* figure he'd found. "What can you tell me about those?"

Sanchez laughed. "David insisted we all carry owl feathers. He'd heard they would help protect us from the police—you know, keep us from getting caught. Juan had owls in his bird cages, so we removed some tail feathers from a couple of great horned owls and carried them with us. It was more to humor David than anything—but who knows, maybe they actually worked. We never got caught. I still have my owl feathers—I kept them as a memento of better times."

"What about *La Santa Muerte*?"

"David carried that *santo* for extra protection from the cops. He believed in her powers. Juan and I didn't go that far."

Rivera thought for a long moment. "Well, I think that answers all my questions." He looked at Bradshaw who shook his head. They stood up.

"I have a question," said Sanchez. "How did you know where to locate me? If you can find me, then so can someone who's out to kill me."

"It's not likely anyone will find you the way I did." Rivera was reluctant to name his source but he figured revealing the story about Rosita would prevent Sanchez from worrying every day about his safety. Rivera smiled. "Rosita told me."

"Rosita?" He looked puzzled. "Rosita doesn't know where I live. She's never been here. How could she tell you?"

Rivera explained the sequence of events that led him to knock on Sanchez's door.

Sanchez laughed. "You know, I really miss my home. I'd love to return to Santa Elena someday and be with my family." He pointed to the framed photographs. "Except for those photographs, I've never laid eyes on Rosita. Every time I talk to her on the phone, she asks me if I'm coming to visit her. It breaks my heart. I want to see her and hug her and spend time with her."

"If we can identify and apprehend the killer, it'll be safe for you to go back home."

"That is a wonderful thought."

Rivera handed him a business card. "Call me if you think of anything else. Anything at all. And don't worry—we won't reveal your location or your new identity."

Rivera and Bradshaw got in the Toyota and headed back to Bradshaw's office.

"Well, that was a productive meeting. Got time for some lunch?" asked Bradshaw.

"I wish I could but I've got to get back to Tierra Amarilla. And I've got an errand to run here in Santa Fe before I leave."

"If you need any help up in Rio Arriba County, don't hesitate to call me. It's not a good idea, you being on your own up there. You call and I'll come."

"Thanks, Sheriff. I really appreciate it."

"It's Leroy."

25

BACK IN HIS own vehicle, Rivera fished out of his shirt pocket the piece of paper on which he'd written the *curandera's* address. His persistent nausea since his encounter with the witch in Santa Elena had been increasing in intensity and now had him continually on edge. Last night, he'd finally called his grandmother, a traditional Hispanic woman, and told her about Rio Arriba County and the *mal ojo* he'd received in Santa Elena. He'd been embarrassed to make the call, since he'd always professed a disbelief in witchcraft, but he was becoming concerned.

"Manny, you must do something right away, before it gets worse," she had said.

"*Abuelita*, I've been taking an antacid to settle my stomach but it hasn't helped at all. Maybe I'm not taking enough."

"That will not help. You must see a *curandera*."

Rivera was familiar with *curanderas*, healing women who used herbs and natural remedies to cure sickness and neutralize curses. A close friend of his grandmother's in Las Cruces was a *curandera*, so he'd grown up with a general awareness of what they did.

"The only healing woman I know lives in Moab. She helped me out on a case a few years ago, but I've never used her curing services," he'd told his grandmother. "I'm in Tierra Amarilla now and heading for Santa Fe tomorrow on business. I'm tired of feeling this way."

She'd said she would do some asking around, find a reputable *curandera* in Santa Fe, and call him back.

An hour later, she'd called with the address of Señora María Veronica Ortiz y Mora. "The Señora is reputed to be a most powerful *curandera*," she said.

After that call, he couldn't very well back out. His grandmother had gone to a lot of trouble to find the right *curandera*. He wasn't about to disappoint his *Abuelita*.

Rivera parked his vehicle in front of a small rock home with a rusted tin roof. It was in an older part of Santa Fe the tourists never visit. There were no art galleries, no upscale restaurants, and no gourmet coffee houses. Just a simple neighborhood with large trees and small houses—a working person's neighborhood. He removed the holster and handgun from under his jacket and placed them in the glove compartment.

He carried a paper bag containing the voodoo dolls he'd collected and knocked on the door. He waited, feeling a little foolish, but he was determined to see it through. The door opened and a small woman stood there with a smile and inquisitive eyes. She was stooped, wrinkled, and wore dark clothing. To Rivera, she didn't look a whole lot different than the witch who had created the problem in the first place.

She led him into a dimly lit living room and pointed to a straight back chair next to a small table. Rivera's nose detected a complex mixture of scents in the air. Across one wall of the room were built-in shelves containing numerous glass containers filled with herbs and powders of various types and colors. The other walls were decorated with framed pictures of *santos* and holy places. A statue he recognized as *El Niño de Atocha* sat on a small table, surrounded by an array of red and white votive candles. He sat down in the chair.

She stood over him and spoke in Spanish. "You are feeling ill, Mr. Policeman?"

Rivera wondered how the *curandera* knew he was a cop. He nodded and told her about the *bruja* in Santa Elena, the face she'd made, and the sound she'd emitted. Then he opened the paper bag and showed her the collection of voodoo dolls. He told her where they had been placed and when. He opened his iPhone and showed her a photo of the witch's curse that had been drawn on the door of his motel room. He was careful to be precise in his descriptions, not knowing what was important and what wasn't.

She nodded. "And what is the nature of your ailment?"

Rivera patted his midsection. "I have been sick in the stomach for several days. It started right after that *bruja* gave me the *mal ojo*."

The *curandera* looked at him for a long moment. "Wait here," she said, and left the room. Rivera heard the sound of a refrigerator door opening and closing. She returned with a bowl of raw eggs and a candle in a brass candleholder. She placed them on the table and left the room a second time. She returned with a plate, a glass half full of water, and a prayer card showing an image of St. Michael. She pulled a book of matches from her pocket and lit the candle. She placed the water glass on the plate and leaned the image of St. Michael against the glass.

"You need a *limpia*," she said. "Please stand up."

Rivera had heard of cleansings administered by *curanderas*. They supposedly cured illness and reversed curses and spells. He could only hope it worked—he was tired of feeling nauseous all the time. He was intensely interested in what the woman was doing but his strong doubts remained. He hoped his doubts wouldn't interfere in some way with the effectiveness of the *limpia*.

She bowed her head and mumbled a prayer that sounded like the Apostle's Creed. She selected an egg from the bowl, stood on tiptoes, and made the sign of the cross above his head with the egg. Then she began moving it in a slow sweeping motion over his head and down his body, front and back. She made a series of crosses at the back of his neck, then worked his shoulders, front and back. She continued sweeping his body, making another cross at his heart and the center of his back. She continued down his body to his abdomen, the palms of his hands, his legs and finally his feet. She stopped and asked him to sit down.

She cracked the egg on the table, pulled apart the shell, and allowed the contents to drop into the glass of water. After it settled, she stared into the glass for a full minute while Rivera watched and wondered what was going on. He remained silent. Finally, the *curandera* pursed her lips and shook her head slightly. She carried the glass into the kitchen and returned with another half-full glass of water.

"Please stand up."

Rivera complied and the *curandera* repeated the process of sweeping his body with a second egg. When she finished, she again broke the egg into the glass of water and studied it for an extended period.

She smiled. "A white line of albumen has encircled the yolk. You should feel better in the morning."

Rivera left his vehicle in the parking lot of the Sanbusco Market Center and headed for the Pranzo Italian Grill, a place where he enjoyed eating whenever he was in Santa Fe. He ordered a glass of Chianti, some garlic bread, and the Penne Bolognese. After dinner, he drove back to Tierra Amarilla, his stomach full and his body relaxed. It might have just been his imagination, but already the queasiness he'd felt in his stomach seemed to be dissipating.

26

THE NEXT MORNING, when Rivera woke up and rolled out of bed, he felt like a new man. The nausea was gone and his stomach was normal again. He found himself wondering if the *curandera* had cured him or the stomach ailment had just run its course. He smiled as he thought about it. He'd always been a staunch nonbeliever in spells and curses, but now he wasn't so sure. Life was full of little surprises.

He left his motel room, fully expecting to find some sort of evil omen hanging on his vehicle, but there was none. Had the witch decided to stop bothering him? Had the *curandera's* magic worked to reverse the curse and discourage the witch? Or was the whole thing just a series of coincidences?

He drove to the Three Ravens Coffee House for breakfast. He parked in the parking lot, walked beneath the raven sculptures, and pushed open the front door. He was surprised to see only a handful of patrons in the restaurant. He thought for a moment, then realized today was Good Friday. It was a day during which devout Catholics would be attending church or spending the day quietly at home. Some would be preparing to attend one of the Penitente processions in remembrance of Christ's crucifixion. In some villages, the Penitentes would go so far as to reenact the crucifixion, using ropes instead of nails to fasten a surrogate to a cross.

After an omelet breakfast and two cups of coffee, he headed for the sheriff's office. He felt it was now time to share everything he knew with Sheriff Gallegos—everything except Victor Sanchez's new identity and his location. That information he would continue to withhold. Perhaps reviewing the case with Gallegos would help Rivera figure out his next step. Despite all the things he'd learned about what had happened fifteen years ago, he remained unable to identify a motive for Archuleta's murder in the LaSals.

From Ruby, Rivera learned that Sheriff Gallegos wouldn't be at the office this morning—more medical problems with his wife—but he would return by early afternoon. And Gloria was out on a domestic disturbance call. That left Jaramillo, now watching Rivera's every move with a surly look, to hold down the fort.

Rivera decided there was nothing he could do until the sheriff returned, so he left the office. He saw the delay as a fortunate opportunity—now he'd be able to drive to Santa Elena and observe the Penitentes' Good Friday procession.

He parked at the edge of town, uncertain whether his presence would be looked upon by the locals as inappropriate. The villagers were gathered on the main street near the church, talking in hushed tones. He strolled toward them and thought for an instant he'd heard the words "stunt driver" uttered by someone in the crowd.

Their eyes were cast upward toward the *morada* where a dozen Penitentes were preparing to start the procession. As he neared the crowd, his eyes fell on Mr. Sanchez who was staring at him with a troubled expression. He was standing at the edge of the crowd with his wife, his daughter, and Rosita. Rosita gave the deputy a shy wave. Mr. Sanchez left the others and approached Rivera.

"May I have a word with you?"

"Of course, Mr. Sanchez."

"In private?" He gestured to a place farther from the crowd.

"Sure." They moved up the street out of earshot.

Sanchez spoke in a whisper. "Victor called me last night after you left his apartment. You must not reveal his whereabouts to anyone. Please. If you do, you will be endangering his life. I'm afraid he will end up like David Archuleta and Juan Baeza."

"Don't worry, Mr. Sanchez. I understand the situation. I won't do anything to endanger Victor."

Sanchez nodded, seeming somewhat reassured. "He is my only son," he added.

Rivera felt like he owed the man a little more hope. "Mr. Sanchez, if I'm able to identify and arrest the killer, Victor will be able to return to Santa Elena and be with his family."

That brought a smile of relief to Sanchez's face. "*Gracias*, Deputy Rivera."

The crowd became silent.

A procession of Penitentes began solemnly descending the hill from the *morada* to the main street. In the lead was a Penitente wearing a black and purple robe and a black hat, riding a shiny sorrel mare with a flaxen mane and tail. He carried a tricolored flag Rivera didn't recognize. Next came the life-sized Christ statue Rivera had seen behind the *morada*. A crown of thorns and rivulets of blood had been added to its head. The Christ figure rested atop a wooden platform carried by four Penitentes wearing red robes. Following them was a Penitente wearing a white robe with a red sash draped over his shoulder. Next came Abelardo Herrera, chief of the Santa Elena *cofradía*, wearing a robe and holding a large crucifix. Behind him followed two young men, barefoot and naked from the waist up. Each held a whip made of natural fiber—yucca, Rivera presumed. They were lashing themselves on the back as they walked. It wasn't just for show—Rivera could hear a snap with each lash of the whips. He winced when they passed by and he could see them from the rear. Blood was trickling down from the raw welts on their backs. The rest of the local Penitentes trailed behind. Rivera recognized Flaco Chavez among them.

The procession turned left on the main street and continued to the end of the road, the people of the village quietly following. Rivera fell in with the group and walked with them. The Penitentes continued on a path which began at the end of the road and led into the hills beyond the village, winding its way through the shade of the tall pines. About every hundred feet, the procession stopped at a Station of the Cross. The Stations were Plexiglas enclosed pictures fastened to posts. The images represented the sequence of events in the crucifixion of Christ, beginning with *Jesus is Condemned to Death.* There would be fourteen of them, Rivera knew, the last being *Jesus is Laid in the Tomb.* At each of the Stations, a brief prayer was recited by Herrera. Beyond the last Station, they came to a small clearing in the forest where a twenty-foot-high cross had been erected. It was constructed of two debarked pine poles and had a white sash draped over the cross arm. A roll of barbed wire was fastened at the intersection of the poles. The people were silent and their heads were bowed. The only sound was the rustling of the trees by a gentle breeze.

Señor Herrera faced the group, welcomed them to *El Calvario,* and led them in a series of prayers. Solemn hymns were sung by the group, accompanied by two villagers who had brought guitars. Rivera recognized the hymns and sang along with the congregation. He was transported to a time in his past when he was a younger man and attended church on a regular basis. The rhythmic tone of the prayers, the community of voices singing the hymns, and the solemnity of the occasion produced in him feelings he hadn't felt in years. He began to experience a sense of belonging to this congregation of villagers. He was among real people in a real community, and began looking at his life as though from above, thinking about the choices he'd made along the way and how those choices had led him to this remote place at this point in time. He had a vague sense that if changes were coming in his life, he was ready to embrace them.

When the congregation finished singing the last hymn, the *cofradía* reassembled the procession and led the people back to the village. Everyone joined together in a final prayer after which the Penitentes thanked the villagers for coming and returned to the *morada*. The congregation slowly broke up and the people began wandering back to their homes. It was a long time before Rivera could bring himself to leave. He stood there alone, now seeing the village through a whole new set of eyes. In a way, he envied these people. They lacked fancy homes, new automobiles, and the latest in computers and designer clothing, but they had a real life.

Rivera spotted Flaco Chavez walking down the hill from the *morada.* Seeing him caused Rivera to remember that he'd failed to ask Flaco a key question during their conversation. The question hadn't occurred to Rivera until after Flaco had driven off from the old *morada.* It had to do with the former sheriff and his sloppy investigation of the Pacheco death.

He approached Flaco with a smile and a friendly wave, hoping he wouldn't spook him into silence.

"Hi, Flaco."

Flaco smiled and nodded.

Rivera pointed up the hill. "Did you rake the morada this morning?"

Flaco smiled. "Of course. I raked both of them."

"God will be happy."

Flaco stifled a laugh. "It's good Friday. Don't make me laugh."

"I forgot to ask you a question when we spoke at the old *morada.*"

"What's that?"

"It's about the former sheriff. Everyone knew you went to the old *morada* each day, right?"

He shrugged. "Sure. I guess so."

"If the sheriff knew that, why do you suppose he didn't come to your home and ask you if you saw anything at the old *morada* the day Angie Pacheco died?"

He shrugged. "I don't think he placed a high value on the lives of the poor people in Rio Arriba County.

If Angie had been from a wealthy family, he would have questioned me and everyone else in the village."

"Did any of his deputies ask you about it?"

"No. The only one who asked me if I saw anything was Eduardo Salazar."

"Eduardo Salazar, the chief of security at the Dominguez estate?"

"That's right. It was after lunch that same day. He came to my home. We always eat a late lunch so I'd say it was about two o'clock. I told him I saw Angie standing by herself at the edge of the bluff and that she was still there when I left. And I told him about those three young men who were having one of their meetings inside the old *morada*."

"How did he react when you told him that?"

"He seemed real interested. He asked me what their names were, so I told him."

"Why do you suppose he was asking these questions?'

Flaco shook his head. "No idea."

27

DRIVING BACK TO the sheriff's office, a clearer picture of what had happened fifteen years ago began to emerge from the murky collection of assorted facts and inferences in Rivera's brain. He tried to get the chronology straight. Angie Pacheco's sister drove her to Santa Elena and dropped her off there. Angie walked a mile or so from the village to the bluff and waited for the baby's father to arrive. Meanwhile, David Archuleta and his two friends were inside the old *morada* cutting and packaging mushrooms. When Flaco arrived at the *morada*, he saw Angie standing alone at the edge of the bluff. He'd also heard the three young men inside the *morada* behind the closed door. He knocked on the door. Victor Sanchez opened it slightly, told Flaco he couldn't come in, and said that it was a private meeting. Victor looked around outside before closing the door and saw Angie standing at the edge of the bluff, apparently waiting there for someone. Flaco finished raking the yard and drove off.

Then what happened? Angie's sister had said that Angie was meeting the father at the bluff for a private discussion about their future. What would that meeting have been about? Marriage, of course. Rivera tried out a few scenarios in his mind. Only one seemed likely. He figured the baby's father had said he wasn't interested in marriage and Angie said she was going to have the baby anyway. An argument ensued and he got mad. He pushed her over the cliff and left.

Rivera pondered that as he drove. It seemed entirely plausible. He wondered about how the baby's father had gotten to the cliff. He must have walked—otherwise the young men inside the *morada* would have heard his vehicle. Later, the three men would exit the *morada*, lock it, see no one, and leave for lunch at Archuleta's home and their meeting in Española later with the drug dealer. Then what?

Eduardo Salazar, chief of security at the Dominguez estate, visited Flaco at his home and asked him if he'd seen anyone at the *morada* that day. Flaco told him he'd seen Angie standing at the bluff. He also told him about the three young men inside the *morada*. Why did Salazar make that inquiry? Perhaps he knew the sheriff wouldn't have done a professional job of investigating the matter.

But wait, something wasn't right. Rivera pulled over onto the shoulder of the road and stopped. Flaco had said Salazar visited his home after lunch—about two o'clock. The hikers hadn't found Angie's body until five o'clock in the afternoon. So how did Salazar know she was dead hours before her body was found? Rivera pounded the steering wheel with the palm of his hand. Of course! Salazar knew because he was the one who had shoved her over the cliff. And that would explain why he had hunted down Archuleta, Baeza, and Sanchez. He wanted to eliminate any possible witnesses.

When Rivera returned to the sheriff's building, he saw Sheriff Gallegos sitting at his desk eating a sandwich. The sheriff waved him into his office. Rivera closed the door as he entered. "We need to talk," he said, now noticing Gilbert Jaramillo getting up from his desk and moving closer.

"What's up?" asked the sheriff.

Rivera glanced at Jaramillo and lowered his voice to a whisper. "Things have pretty much fallen into place in my investigation. I believe I know who killed David Archuleta."

Gallegos put down his sandwich. "Just a minute."

He stepped outside the office and spoke to Jaramillo. Jaramillo nodded his head enthusiastically, picked up his hat, and left the building.

Gallegos returned to the office and closed the door. "I just sent Gilbert to the courthouse to pick up some papers." He smiled. "I told him it was important. Gilbert likes to do important things. Now, who do you think killed David Archuleta?"

"Eduardo Salazar, chief of security at the Dominguez estate."

Gallegos looked incredulous. "Oh, come on. That can't be right. Eduardo is a respected man in the community. What possible reason would he have for killing a young man held in high regard as a Penitente?"

"I think Salazar was having an affair with Angie Pacheco and got her pregnant. Eduardo was married and when he learned his girlfriend was expecting, he panicked. He didn't want his wife to find out and he certainly didn't want Don Fernando Dominguez to hear about it. From what I've gathered, Don Fernando wouldn't put up with infidelity or any other indiscretion on the part of a resident of his estate. Angie wanted to have the child whether or not Salazar married her. Salazar couldn't risk Angie talking about it or confiding in someone, so he arranged to meet her at the bluff to talk about things. He shoved her over the cliff."

"Maybe, but what's that got to do with Archuleta?"

"Afterwards, Salazar realized that Flaco Chavez had been up there that day raking the yard at the old *morada*. He became worried that Flaco might have seen what he'd done. He visited Flaco and learned that he had departed while Angie was still standing at the bluff, alive and well. He'd also learned that Archuleta, Baeza, and Sanchez were inside the *morada* having some kind of meeting. Actually, they were slicing and packaging psychedelic mushrooms they'd collected in the forest.

Later they would drive to Española to sell them to a dealer from Albuquerque. By the way, they weren't users—they used the profits from their mushroom business to help needy villagers in Santa Elena.

"That was the last mushroom crop from the Tusas Mountains because of lack of rainfall, so the next day they headed to the LaSal Mountains in Utah where there had been recent rain. Salazar must have followed them looking for an opportunity to eliminate them as possible witnesses to Angie's murder. He killed Archuleta but the other two returned to Santa Elena safely before he could get to them. He killed Baeza a couple of days later down here and no doubt was planning to kill Sanchez too, but Sanchez got scared and disappeared. Sanchez assumed their drug buyer or one of his competitors had a reason to eliminate the three of them, but he was wrong. It was Salazar. Salazar wanted to eliminate any possible witnesses to his crime."

Gallegos smiled and lit a cigarette. He snapped closed his cigarette lighter and blew out a plume of smoke. "Can you prove any of this?"

"That's where you come in, Sheriff. We need a search warrant for Salazar's residence and vehicle. I think we'll find a .30 caliber rifle and I think it'll be a match for the bullets removed from Archuleta and Baeza. Also, we need to exhume Angie Pacheco's body and get a sample of the fetus's DNA—then compare it to Salazar's DNA."

Gallegos turned his palms up. "But all this is just conjecture. What facts do you have to back it up?"

Rivera sat back. "Everything is based on interviews—including one I had with Victor Sanchez. Fortunately, I was able to locate and question him. For his own safety, I won't reveal his whereabouts. The key fact is that Salazar visited Flaco Chavez asking about possible witnesses hours before Angie's body was found."

"He might have had some other reason for asking."

"Like what? Her body hadn't been found yet. How could he possibly have known she was dead?"

Gallegos took a drag on his cigarette. "No idea, but you're just guessing that was his reason for visiting Flaco."

"What other reason could there be?"

"Who knows? Look. All this happened fifteen years ago. Why stir up the whole community now?"

Rivera could see the sheriff was getting nervous at the thought of doing anything that might disrupt life on Don Fernando's estate. "My job is to apprehend David Archuleta's murderer."

"You want me to go to a judge and get a search warrant and an exhumation order?"

"Yes."

"Today is Good Friday. There won't be a judge at the courthouse."

"Contact one of them at home."

"No. First of all, that'll get me fired. And secondly, that's not the right way to do it."

"Not the right way to do it? What do you mean?"

"If we want to search a home on the Dominguez estate, we must first get permission from Don Fernando himself. He would consider it disrespectful if we went to a judge."

"Disrespectful? You've got to be kidding, Sheriff. This is a murder case."

"Manny, you're out of your jurisdiction. We'll have to do it my way."

"Which is what?"

"We must request a meeting with Don Fernando. I believe he would grant us one if we told him it was important."

"He'll want to know what the meeting is about before he agrees to it. As soon as you tell him, that rifle will disappear in an instant."

Gallegos frowned. "No. Don Fernando is one of the finest, most ethical, most religious men you'll ever meet. He's never been known to lie, cheat, or steal." Gallegos's tone was almost one of scolding. He was all but shaking his finger at Rivera. "His reputation is impeccable. His wealth is a result of being lucky enough to have been born into the right family, not because of some crooked dealings. You can bet your life on his fairness."

"So what do you propose? That I call him and request an appointment?"

"No, dammit. I'll make the call. Your hunch was right about the two slugs being a match, and your new theory seems plausible, so I'll go along with you even though I think this is a big mistake." He thought for a long moment. "This is probably gonna cost me my goddamn job." He opened his desk drawer and stubbed out his cigarette in the ashtray.

"Do you know the Don personally?"

"No. One time I was hired for extra security at some big political function being held outdoors at the estate. He was sitting with the governor at a table about fifty feet from my post. That's as close as I've ever gotten to the man."

Rivera watched as Sheriff Gallegos made the call. The sheriff explained to Don Fernando's secretary that an important matter had come up and he needed to meet with Don Fernando. He apparently wasn't asked about the subject of the meeting. Thankfully, saying it was important was sufficient for the Don to grant the sheriff an audience.

Gallegos hung up the phone. "We have an appointment in one hour. We should leave here in thirty minutes."

28

JUST AS RIVERA and Sheriff Gallegos were leaving the sheriff's building, Gilbert Jaramillo was returning from the courthouse with a file in his hand.

"I heard you're going out to the Dominguez estate," said Jaramillo, confronting Gallegos.

Rivera was impressed at how fast word traveled in Rio Arriba County. Probably someone at the estate had called someone at the courthouse who told the janitor who saw Jaramillo in the hallway and told him.

"I want to come with you."

"No. You stay in the office," said the sheriff.

"I'm coming along," said Jaramillo, as though there was no question about it.

"What for?" asked the sheriff.

"He's my uncle. I should be there."

The sheriff was silent for a long moment. Rivera knew what he was thinking. Jaramillo would lose face if he weren't part of the contingent visiting the Don. After all, Jaramillo lived on the estate along with many of Don Fernando's other relatives. And not bringing the nephew might be viewed as a slight to the Don.

"Alright, Gilbert. You follow along behind us in your unit. You can attend the meeting, but don't talk. Understood?"

Jaramillo nodded. "Alright."

The two vehicles approached the entrance of the Dominguez estate, the sheriff driving the first unit with Rivera as a passenger, and Jaramillo following in the second unit. They turned off the gravel county road onto the paved two-lane driveway of the estate, passing through the mammoth rock entryway. The driveway meandered across an expanse of meadow before rising into the darkness of a pine forest. Just beyond the crest of a hill, they passed a man wearing a panama hat and a white guayabera shirt. He was sitting in a chair in the shade of the trees, a rifle resting across his lap. He waved the vehicles through and then spoke into his radio. Rivera found it interesting that the guard was not visible from the road to Santa Elena but was located well into the property, beyond the sight of Santa Elena residents passing by. Was keeping the guard hidden intended to give the estate a friendlier appearance?

They passed through the pines and descended into a large, open valley. At the far end of the valley, Rivera could see a large, two-story Spanish style home, a mansion in Rivera's estimation. Its walls were tan stucco and its roof tiles were red. Rivera guessed it contained about twenty rooms. On their right, they passed a paved street ending in a cul-de-sac with a dozen smaller homes, miniature versions of the mansion, and each one much finer than the best house in Santa Elena.

Gallegos pointed. "Those are the homes of Don Fernando's relatives and close associates. That first one is where Eduardo Salazar and his family live. Gilbert Jaramillo lives in the one across the street." He produced a humorless chuckle. "Gilbert's house is twice the size of the one I live in."

"Gloria told me that Josefina, the *bruja*, lives out here too," said Rivera.

"That's right. I'm told she lives alone in a cabin in the woods somewhere. The Don looks after her for some reason."

As they got closer to the mansion, Rivera could see that his estimate of the number of rooms it contained had been too low. He adjusted it to thirty rooms. The lawn around the house looked like a golf course fairway and the bushes and trees surrounding it were professionally manicured. Behind the edifice were a huge patio, two lighted tennis courts, and an Olympic-size swimming pool.

Several women watched over ten or twelve children playing on the lawn next to the mansion. The kids were enjoying themselves on colorful slides, climbing bars, and trampolines. Four dogs were prancing after a boy who was laughing and running with a ball. Rivera noticed how much better dressed these kids were than the ones living in Santa Elena.

"Don Fernando loves his family, especially his grandkids and great-grandkids," said Gallegos. "I've heard he spends a lot of his time playing with them. And the children on the estate love him. They call him Papi Don."

"This place must have cost a fortune to build," said Rivera.

"Sure. But that moly mine on the Don's property is highly profitable. I saw a magazine article about ten years ago that said it was worth over two hundred million dollars. It's probably worth a lot more than that today. Don Fernando lucked out when his ancestors were awarded the land grant for this property."

The two vehicles stopped directly in front of the house. A large, Hispanic man dressed in pressed jeans, a white shirt, and a western jacket was waiting for the visitors. Rivera noted the bulge under his jacket and sized him up as a bodyguard. The man welcomed them and politely requested that they follow him. The contingent of visitors walked up a wide stairway, through the front door of the house, and into a vestibule that was larger than the sheriff's building. The floors were tiled, the ceiling high, and the room furnished with antique tables and chairs. A giant, glittering chandelier hung from the ceiling. Stairs on each side of the lobby curved up to the second floor. The mansion was quiet except for the sound of their heels clicking on the tile floor and the muffled laughter of the children playing outside.

They followed their escort up the stairs and into a library with built-in bookcases and an elaborately appointed antique desk. A man Rivera assumed was Don Fernando was seated in a chair in front of the desk. The chair was made of hand-carved mahogany wood and was upholstered with maroon velvet cushioning. Three matching chairs had been set up facing him. There was a step in the library floor so that the Don's chair was about six inches above his visitors' chairs.

With a sweep of his hand, their escort motioned for them to sit in the chairs. Then he closed the library door and positioned himself in the back of the room. Sitting at a side desk was a handsome Hispanic woman, obviously the Don's secretary.

There were no handshakes. The Don sat motionless, his forearms resting easily on the arms of the chair. He was impeccably dressed in black trousers, a white shirt, and a dark blue western-cut jacket with white stitching. A bolo tie with a silver clasp hung around his neck. He was a slender man with dark eyes and thick, gray hair. His expression was neutral and revealed nothing about what he was thinking.

The sheriff sat in the center chair with Rivera on his left and Jaramillo on his right. Rivera wondered how they knew to put out three chairs. He figured the guard at the entrance must have called ahead with the head count.

"Welcome to my home, Ruben," said the Don, looking down at his visitors. "How may I help you?" His tone of voice was neutral and measured.

Rivera noticed the Don had addressed Gallegos as Ruben instead of Sheriff Gallegos—not in a condescending way, but in a tone and manner reserved for the help.

"Thank you for seeing us, Don Fernando," said the sheriff. He gestured toward Rivera. "I'd like to introduce..."

"Yes, of course," said the Don. "Deputy Sheriff Manuel Rivera from Grand County, Utah." He looked at Rivera. "Welcome, Deputy Rivera."

"Thank you, Don Fernando." Rivera felt at a disadvantage. He had the uncomfortable feeling that Don Fernando knew everything about him.

"I understand you are seeking the person who murdered David Archuleta."

"Yes, I am. I have reason to believe we've identified the killer."

Don Fernando looked at the sheriff with raised eyebrows. "Is that so, Ruben?"

"Yes, Don Fernando." The sheriff's voice had a higher pitch than normal and its timbre had changed. His tension was obvious. He cleared his throat. "Do you remember David Archuleta? He lived in Santa Elena.

He was a Penitente there. A good man. He disappeared fifteen years ago." The sheriff began relating in wearisome detail the story about Mrs. Foster and the items found in the barn.

The Don cut him off. "I'm aware that a corpse found in the LaSal Mountains around that time was recently identified as David Archuleta." He glanced for an instant at Gilbert Jaramillo and the corners of his mouth turned up a few millimeters. He shifted his gaze to Rivera. "I also understand that the weapon that killed him was the same one that killed Juan Baeza."

Rivera figured the Don was a man who didn't like to waste time. He was cutting through all the preliminaries so the sheriff would get to the point. Jaramillo's eavesdropping activities had likely been the primary source of his information. No sense telling the Don things he already knew.

Rivera decided to take over the conversation so Gallegos wouldn't drag it out. "That's correct, Don Fernando. Archuleta and Baeza were killed with the same .30 caliber rifle. They and their friend Victor Sanchez had regular jobs, but they also had a side business—they harvested psychedelic mushrooms in the mountains and sold them to a drug dealer from Albuquerque. They used the money to help the people of Santa Elena. Archuleta was searching for mushrooms when he was killed in the LaSals. Baeza was killed here in the Tusas Mountains a couple of days later, then Sanchez got frightened and left town. At first I thought maybe Sanchez had killed his partners over some disagreement about money. But then I was able to contact him and learn the whole story."

The Don glanced at Jaramillo who shrugged slightly.

"I'd understood that after Victor Sanchez mysteriously left town, no one had heard from him again. How were you able to locate him?"

"Forgive me, Don Fernando. I'm not able to reveal that because of a promise I made to Sanchez." Rivera was careful not to let it show on his face, but he resented having to kowtow to the Don. He couldn't believe he'd just said *Forgive me, Don Fernando.* The Don should be down at the sheriff's office answering questions, not sitting up there asking them. But this was Rio Arriba County, not Grand County, Utah.

The Don smiled slightly. "Yes, I understand. Please go on, Deputy Rivera."

"A few days before Archuleta was killed, Angie Pacheco, a girl from Canjilon, died from a fall off a bluff overlooking Estaca Canyon. She was seventeen, unmarried, and pregnant. She was waiting at the bluff to talk to the father. According to her sister, she was going to have the baby no matter what, but she hoped the father would decide to marry her. Instead, he came to the bluff and shoved her over. That was around noon that day. He later learned the three young men had been inside the old *morada* that same day. They were possible witnesses and therefore represented a threat."

"And you're saying, because of that possibility, he set out to kill all three of them?"

"Yes."

"How did he learn they were inside the old *morada*?"

"He visited the home of Flaco Chavez about two o'clock that same day, and asked Flaco if he had seen anyone up there while he was raking the *morada* yard."

"Ah, yes. I've met Flaco. A gentle soul and a devout Penitente."

"Flaco told his visitor that he'd seen the girl standing by the cliff alone when he left. He also told him about the three men in the *morada*."

"Perhaps this man was just interested. When he heard about the girl, maybe he was just curious."

"Don Fernando, her body was found by hikers that day around five o'clock."

The Don sat motionless, eyes almost closed, as though processing everything he'd heard, testing the inferences, looking for flaws. Finally, he opened his eyes widely and focused them on Rivera. "And now you are going to tell me the name of this man?"

Rivera looked at the sheriff. He was motionless and staring straight ahead, his fingers tightly gripping the arms of his chair. Next to him, Jaramillo sat watching Rivera, eyes wide open in anticipation.

"That man is Eduardo Salazar, your chief of security," said Rivera.

Don Fernando leaned forward, frowning. "Eduardo? Why Eduardo has lived his entire life on this estate. So did his father and grandfather. You must be mistaken. Eduardo is a happily married man whose children play with my grandchildren. This is outrageous. What proof do you have of this?"

The sheriff started to respond but Rivera cut him off. "We need your help with the proof, Don Fernando. Archuleta and Baeza were shot with the same rifle. We want to search Salazar's home and vehicle and confiscate any .30 caliber rifles he owns in order to perform ballistics testing on them. We would like to do that immediately. Later, we will exhume the body of Angie Pacheco and compare the DNA of her fetus to that of Eduardo Salazar. That will prove he's the father of the child."

"You said that girl was seventeen?"

"Seventeen, yes. She was class vice president at her high school."

The Don sat back in his chair and thought for a full minute in silence. The only sound was the ticking of an antique clock hanging on the wall. Sheriff Gallegos shifted in his chair while Jaramillo sat frozen, staring at the Don. Finally, the Don spoke, looking directly at the sheriff. "Ruben, if you do these things and it turns out you're wrong, what will you do then?"

"I'll apologize to you and Eduardo and his family. That's all I can offer. Don Fernando, I'm just trying to do what a good sheriff would do," he said in a plaintive voice.

Another long pause. Don Fernando turned to his secretary. "Contact Eduardo and ask him to join me immediately. Don't tell him what the meeting is about." He turned to the security man in the back of the room and addressed him. "Say nothing of this to anyone."

The guard bowed his head slightly. "Yes, Don Fernando."

The secretary picked up a portable radio and spoke with Salazar, then turned to the Don. "He's on his horse, about two miles out, Don Fernando. He's on his way."

29

NOT A WORD was spoken while they waited. Don Fernando sat rigid in his chair, staring straight ahead, while Interim Sheriff Ruben Gallegos sat with folded arms, sweating and looking uncomfortable. Finally, there were three knocks on the library door. Don Fernando motioned for the guard to open it. Eduardo Salazar entered the room and the guard closed the door behind him. The guard had set up a chair for Salazar to the Don's left, directly across from the secretary, so that all parties could see one other.

"Please have a seat, Eduardo."

Eduardo walked to the empty chair. His expression was serious and his manner deferential. He glanced at Rivera with a look of concern and then sat down.

"Eduardo, you have lived your entire life on the Dominguez estate, just as your father did and his father before him. During that time, you have been loyal to me and your services here have been exemplary and indispensable. Your wife and children grace these lands and add joy to my life. I thank you for your many years of faithful service."

"Don Fernando, it has been an honor for me to serve you."

"Now, I must ask you about a matter that concerns me. I expect total honesty in your answers." The Don's tone was matter-of-fact and business-like.

"Yes, of course, Don Fernando." Salazar's eyes were wide open and locked onto the Don.

"We have been discussing the death of Angie Pacheco fifteen years ago. She was seventeen when she died. A good girl, from what I'm told. You would have been about thirty-five years old back then. Were you having an affair with Angie Pacheco?

Salazar's mouth dropped open. He sat back in his chair with a dumbfounded look on his face. "Why no, Don Fernando, I've always been a happily married man. I'm devoted to my wife and family."

"You've always been honest with me, Eduardo. You must tell me the truth."

Eduardo pleaded. "I am telling the truth, Don Fernando."

"You spoke with Flaco Chavez early in the afternoon the day the Pacheco girl died. You asked him if he had seen anyone besides her at the old *morada* that day. Is that true?"

Salazar thought for a moment. "Yes, I believe I recall that."

"Why were you asking him that question?"

Salazar hesitated. His left thumb twitched. "Because I was interested in what had happened to that girl."

"The girl's body wasn't found until five o'clock—three hours later. Yet you were asking your questions early in the afternoon. How do you explain that?"

Eduardo looked at the others in the room. A sheen of perspiration had appeared on his face. He shifted in his seat. "Don Fernando, may I answer you in private? This is not a matter for the ears of outsiders."

The Don's voice became stern. "Answer me now. You were asking Flaco Chavez about possible witnesses even before that young girl's body was found. You pushed her over the cliff, didn't you?"

"Don Fernando, please."

"Answer me."

Salazar fell to his knees and clasped his hands together. "Don Fernando, please permit me to speak with you in private."

"No, Eduardo, you killed her, didn't you? And then you killed David Archuleta and Juan Baeza to eliminate possible witnesses. Isn't that right?"

"Don Fernando, we must speak privately. Please."

"The authorities have the slugs from the two shootings. They wish to test your rifle and compare it to the two slugs. I am going to allow them to do that. Now tell me, what will they find?"

"Please, Don Fernando. Don't do this." Salazar's face was ashen and his eyes darted around the room, as if searching for a credible answer.

The Don stood up, angry and shaking. "Answer me," he said in a booming voice.

Salazar was silent for a long moment, staring in apparent disbelief at the Don. Then he covered his face with his hands and began trembling. "Yes, Don Fernando. I killed them all."

The Don pointed a finger at Salazar. "Thou shalt not kill, Eduardo Salazar. Thou shalt not kill. Sheriff Gallegos, arrest this man."

Gallegos turned to Jaramillo. "Cuff him, Gilbert."

"Yessir, Sheriff," he said. He pulled the cuffs from his belt, snapped them on Salazar's wrists, and read him his rights.

Rivera had never seen anything like it. Salazar's loyalty to the Don and his respect for him were so strong that he chose to incriminate himself in front of witnesses rather than tell the Don a lie. Rivera imagined that's the way things must have been two hundred years ago in Spain. Even murderers had a sense of honor. He also noticed that the Don now addressed Gallegos as Sheriff Gallegos instead of Ruben. He must have decided Gallegos would make a good sheriff after all. It appeared to Rivera that, in that instant, Don Fernando had anointed Gallegos as permanent sheriff and, as a result, Jaramillo had accepted Gallegos as his boss. It was remarkable to behold.

The sheriff and Jaramillo marched Salazar out of the library. Rivera lingered a moment and spoke to the Don. "I'm sorry to have brought so much grief into your life."

The Don's eyes were moist but he held his head high. "You did the right thing."

30

IT WAS THREE O'CLOCK in the afternoon and Rivera was famished. He headed for the Three Ravens Coffee House for a late lunch while Sheriff Gallegos and Deputy Jaramillo brought Eduardo Salazar to the sheriff's office for processing. Rivera ordered a panini sandwich, a couple of brownies, and a cup of coffee.

He wolfed down the sandwich and the first brownie, then slowed down as he started on the second brownie. He took a sip of coffee and sat back, thinking about what had happened today. David Archuleta's killer had finally been apprehended, fifteen years after he'd committed his crime. A few days ago, Rivera had wondered if he'd ever be able to solve the crime. Today, he had his man.

He thought about Salazar—a happily married man with a family and a great job, living in a fine home in a paradise-like environment. Why would he risk all that to have an affair with a seventeen-year-old girl? In a small village like Santa Elena, the chances of discovery were much higher than they would be in a large city. Yet he took that chance. Rivera shook his head.

His thoughts shifted to Don Fernando. Rivera had never met anyone like him. He was good to the people living on his estate. Life there must be idyllic for his family members and employees. That is, unless they violated the Don's sense of right and wrong or displayed a lack of loyalty. Then he would come down on them swiftly and powerfully, like an archangel smiting the wicked. Salazar knew that but he confessed anyway. Rivera figured one of the .30 caliber rifles confiscated from his home was the murder weapon—a test was being expedited and the results would be known shortly—so Salazar realized he'd been caught. There was no way out, so he confessed to the Don. But why do that? Why not wait until the case had been proven? Was it a sense of honor? Or was it because Salazar wanted the Don to continue caring for his family while Salazar was in prison? That had to be it. With Salazar in jail, his family would have no means of support without Don Fernando's generosity.

Rivera finished lunch and walked toward the sheriff's office. It was a beautiful day with a blue sky and a warm sun. He thought about taking a couple of days off, now that his job was done. He could spend some time here in the mountains and perhaps go hiking and explore this beautiful country. He had a desire to drive back to Santa Elena and see if he could get to know the people a little better. The village seemed to be pulling at him like a magnet and he wanted to spend some more time there. Somehow, while he'd been occupied hunting down a murderer, he'd gotten hooked on the little village and its residents. That made him think about Victor Sanchez and his father. He stopped outside the sheriff's office and dialed Victor's number.

"Hello?"

"Victor, this is Deputy Sheriff Rivera calling."

"Uh. Yes?"

"We've arrested the man who killed David and Juan. You can come home now."

"Really? Oh, my God, that makes me so happy." Rivera could tell by the tone of Victor's voice that he was thrilled. "I've been wanting to introduce my fiancé to my parents and show her where I grew up. Thank you so much, Deputy Rivera."

Rivera smiled. "You're welcome."

"Who was it that killed my friends?"

Rivera told him the story about Salazar and Angie Pacheco.

"Eduardo? I'm surprised. He always seemed like a straight-up kind of man. We all looked up to him. I guess you never know about people."

Rivera wished Victor the best, clicked off, and entered the sheriff's office. Ruby was the first to congratulate him, touching him on the arm and smiling her flirty smile.

Then Gilbert Jaramillo came over with an embarrassed expression. He smiled, shook Rivera's hand without a word, and returned to his desk. It was the first time Rivera had seen him without a scowl.

Rivera knocked on Sheriff Gallegos's door and entered.

"Good job, Manny."

"Thanks. And thanks very much for your help."

"I'm the one who should be thanking you. Since our meeting with Don Fernando, I've had calls from all three county commissioners. They want me to run for sheriff at the next election. I guess the Don has given me his imprimatur."

"You'll make an excellent sheriff." Rivera lowered himself into a chair. "I can't stop thinking about the meeting we had with Don Fernando. He's an unusual man. He runs that estate like it's a country and he's the king."

"That's the way it is around here. The people hold him in the highest regard. He's probably the greatest asset this county has."

"And Salazar is an interesting fellow too. I'm trying to understand why he confessed so easily."

"He knew we had him. In fact, the ballistics test results were emailed to me fifteen minutes ago. Salazar's rifle fired the bullets that killed those two young men. I've informed him of that."

"What did he say?"

"He just nodded and admitted everything again. He said now there would be no need to dig up that girl's body and perform a DNA analysis on the fetus."

"Really? That's an odd comment."

"Around here, people are either afraid of corpses or they worship them. The whole idea of death preoccupies them. Who knows what he was thinking? Anyway, not exhuming her body will save the county some money."

Rivera was curious about what made a man like Salazar tick. "I'd like to talk with him for a minute. Try to understand him better."

"Sure. Go ahead. He's in the holding cell in the back of the building. It's a temporary facility until our new building is finished."

Rivera walked back to the holding cell. It was a ten-foot square room constructed of lumber and a double layer of heavy wire mesh. Salazar was sitting motionless on a bench, his forearms resting on his thighs. His head was hanging down and he was staring at the cement floor. Rivera dragged a chair over to the cell.

"Señor Salazar. Would you indulge me for a moment? I'd like to ask you about something."

Salazar looked up, his dark countenance made darker by bloodshot eyes. He looked like he'd been crying. "Yes, what is it?"

"I'm wondering why you confessed to three murders so readily. This is something I'm not used to seeing.

Most people who commit murder deny it to the end. It takes incontrovertible proof to convict them. You didn't even wait for us to prove it."

He shrugged and returned his gaze to the floor. "I was stupid. I should have disposed of the rifle. Instead, I hid it above the ceiling in the security office. It was my favorite hunting rifle and I wanted to keep it. After a few years, I figured it was safe to take it down. I removed it from the security office and put it back in my den. I knew you'd have the proof as soon as you searched my house."

"What about the girl?"

"What about her?"

"It would take us a long time to prove she was carrying your baby. And maybe we couldn't get the proof at all. Maybe the fetus had decomposed too much. Why admit to killing her?'

"What's the difference? Proving I killed two people or three people doesn't seem to matter much. I'll be in prison for the rest of my life."

"The sheriff said he might not exhume Angie's body."

"There's no point to it. I've admitted I killed her. Why put her family through all that? It would be like reliving her death."

"Did you know her family?"

"No. But no family would want to go through that twice."

Rivera was baffled. He knew avoiding an exhumation would be a good thing for all concerned, but why would Angie's killer be so concerned about her family? Angie must not have meant much to him. A summer fling, maybe. If he cared so little about her, why show all this concern for her family? Rivera wondered if he'd ever understand how the people living in these mountain villages thought about things. "You have a strong loyalty to Don Fernando. Is that why you wouldn't lie to him about the killings?"

"Most people don't understand about loyalty. To those of us living on the estate, it's a way of life. We'd all die for that man."

Rivera stood up. "I must say I'm impressed with the depth of your loyalty."

"I've been in charge of protecting the Don, his family, and the estate for all of my adult life. He is the reason I had a life at all. And I mean that literally. When I was a baby, I became very sick. The local doctor told my parents I wouldn't live. Don Fernando personally drove me and my family to a facility in Albuquerque where they had the doctors and medical staff to diagnose and cure me. He stayed there until I was well. Ever since then, he's taken care of me and my family. He uses the money from the moly mine to look after all his people. Years ago, when my father was hurt working in the mine, Don Fernando kept paying him, even though he was unable to work for several years. That's what loyalty is all about."

Rivera left Salazar and returned to the sheriff's office.

"You satisfied?" asked the sheriff, standing and coming around from behind his desk.

Rivera tumbled the question around in his mind. "Not really. Something doesn't sit right with me." He laughed. "But I can't figure out what it is. Maybe I'm just used to a different class of criminals."

The sheriff slapped him on the back. "You worry too much, Manny. It's near quitting time. Let's go have a beer."

31

RIVERA SLID INTO a corner booth in the back of Arturo's Lounge. Sheriff Gallegos sat down across from him. The place was small and dimly lit. It had a wood floor and an old-fashioned oak bar with a brass foot rail. Behind the bar was a large mirror with a neon Budweiser sign. Below that were cascading shelves containing a wide selection of liquor bottles. The place smelled like stale beer. Rivera and Gallegos were the only customers.

"*Buenas tardes,* Ruben." said the bartender. He was a small man with gray hair, a gray moustache, and a brown, wrinkled face. "Or should I say Sheriff Gallegos? Congratulations. I heard the good news."

"Hi, Arturo. And thanks, but it won't be official until the election." The sheriff turned to Rivera. "What'll you have, Manny? The county is buying."

"Thanks. Make mine a Miller Lite."

"Two Miller Lites, Arturo."

Arturo brought two longneck bottles and a bowl of peanuts, placed them on the table with a couple of paper napkins, and returned to the bar.

Gallegos raised his bottle in a toast. "Well, it's been an interesting week." He took a swig.

Rivera nodded, took a drink, and set his bottle down.

Gallegos looked at him. "Something's bothering you, Manny. What is it?"

Rivera laughed. "You're right. Something *is* bothering me. I think it has to do with Salazar not wanting Angie Pacheco's body exhumed. He mentioned it to you and then he went on and on with me about how it wouldn't be fair to make her family relive the tragedy."

"What's wrong with that?"

"For one thing, he didn't know Angie's family. For another, he was worrying about something that was relatively inconsequential compared to his own problems. It just doesn't seem right to me."

"Got any theories?"

Rivera put his bottle on the table and leaned back. "I think we should go ahead with the exhumation and the DNA analysis."

"Why?"

"Because I'm not sure Salazar was the father of Angie's child. I think he might be covering for someone else."

"Who?"

"Maybe the Don himself."

Gallegos almost choked on his beer. He lowered his bottle to the table with a look of exasperation on his face. "I can't believe you said that. That's the craziest idea I've ever heard. Dammit Rivera, I just made sheriff. Now you're trying to screw it up for me."

Rivera grinned. "It's just a hunch but it's possible Salazar is covering for someone."

"Why would Salazar cop to a murder he didn't commit?"

"He's going to prison for the Archuleta and Baeza murders—probably two life sentences. So a third murder wouldn't affect him at all. Three life sentences are the same as two."

"But what does he have to gain?"

"The Don will take care of his family for him."

Gallegos thought for a long moment, then shook his head. "The Don's wife was alive back then. They were very close and he wasn't the type to be cheating on her. At least, that's what I think. It doesn't fit. And I'll be damned if I'm going to jeopardize my new job by accusing him of murder based on one of your hunches."

"What about the exhumation, just to be sure about things?"

Gallegos thought for a moment. "I don't think so. It'll stir up the whole community if I ask the Don for a saliva sample for a DNA comparison. No, that's not a good idea. You've got your killer. You can go back to

Moab with your head held high. If I look like I'm accusing the Don of a crime, my head will be held high too—at the end of a rope."

Rivera smiled. "Still, it's an interesting possibility, isn't it?"

"I should know by now not to doubt your hunches but this one is too far out. There's no proof here, only your sense of why Salazar was concerned about an exhumation. I can't do it."

Deputy Gloria Valdez entered the bar and sat down next to Rivera. She had a look of concern on her face.

"Want a beer, Gloria?" asked the sheriff.

"No thanks. I came here to tell you that Dolores Salazar, Eduardo's wife, just came into the office. She's asked to see her husband. She's talking to Gilbert now, waiting for an answer. I wasn't sure if that would create a problem with the District Attorney so I thought I'd better check with you. Is it okay if she visits him?"

"I'm not sure either. I'd better go talk to her myself," said the sheriff. He chugged the last of his beer and stood up. "Want to come along, Manny?"

"Sure."

The three of them left the bar and headed back to the office.

A pickup truck with four children sitting in its bed was parked in front of the sheriff's building. They sat quietly, staring straight ahead like they were in a state of shock.

"Those are the Salazar children," whispered Gloria.

Inside the office, Mrs. Salazar was talking to Deputy Sheriff Gilbert Jaramillo. She was crying and obviously distraught. When she saw the sheriff, she stood up and spoke to him in a plaintive voice.

"I need to see my husband," she said. "Please, Señor Sheriff. Don Fernando has evicted us from the estate. He said he does not want the family of a murderer living on his land."

So much for loyalty, thought Rivera. He remembered Gloria's words from a few days ago. *No one gets a second chance to disrespect the Don.* It seemed a cruel thing to do.

"When does he want you out of there?" asked the sheriff.

"Right away. They're packing up our things now. We have no place to go. Please let me speak to my husband. I don't know what to do."

Gloria spoke up. "I know of an empty house in La Puente. The people who lived there abandoned it years ago. It needs some cleaning up but it'll do until you can find something better."

"But we have no furniture. The Don said he owned the house *and* the furniture. We were forced to leave with only our clothing and personal things."

"I'll make some calls," said Gloria. "I'm sure we can get some furniture donated by T.A. residents, or at least on a loan basis. I'll handle it."

"Oh, thank you, Deputy Valdez. That's a big relief. We can live there until we rent a house somewhere. We have some money saved so we'll be okay for a while. I'll need to find a job and my older son will have to quit school and go to work too." She looked at Sheriff Gallegos. "I'd still like to visit my husband, just to talk to him. I know he must feel very lonely now."

"Let me call the D.A. and see if it's okay," said the sheriff.

Gallegos went to his office and made the call. When he returned, he spoke softly to Mrs. Salazar. "I'm very sorry, but the District Attorney wants to question your husband before he speaks with you or anyone else connected with the case. Tomorrow morning would be a better time." He turned to Gloria. "Why don't you drive over to that house in La Puente now and show it to Mrs. Salazar? She can follow you in her vehicle. I'll send over a couple of county maintenance people to help clean the place up."

"Let's go see the house now," said Gloria, putting her arm around Mrs. Salazar. "You can follow me there." She led her out of the building.

Rivera followed Gallegos into his office. The sheriff sat down behind his desk, massaging his temples with his fingertips. He looked emotionally exhausted.

"That poor woman," said Rivera. "She deserves better treatment than that. One thing's for sure, though. Don Fernando was not the father of Angie Pacheco's child. If he was, he'd never have booted Salazar's family off the estate."

"Yeah. If Salazar was taking the murder rap for the Don, the Don would do everything he could to help Salazar's family."

"Maybe Salazar is protecting someone else. Let's go visit him. When he learns what happened to his family, he might become a little more talkative."

"Alright."

32

SHERIFF GALLEGOS SPOKE in soft tones as he described to Eduardo Salazar what the Don had done to his family. He explained that Gloria was taking them to an abandoned house in La Puente and that furniture donations would be solicited from the community.

Rivera watched Salazar's face as he attempted to digest the news. Salazar had been abandoned by the man he loved and looked up to, and now suffered the humiliation of his family being forced to move from a plush home on the Dominguez estate to an abandoned house in a small village.

Salazar appeared incredulous the whole time the sheriff talked. He stood up and gripped the wire mesh of his cell with his fingertips. "I can't believe this. Is this some kind of a trick?"

"It's true," said Gallegos. I just spoke to your wife."

Salazar looked at Rivera.

Rivera nodded.

Salazar sat down. "I don't believe what you're saying. The Don would never do anything like that to me," he said. "Let me talk to my wife. I want to hear it directly from her."

"The D.A. won't allow visitors until after he questions you. You can talk to your wife tomorrow morning."

"Then let me talk to Gilbert. He's my neighbor. I've known him since we were kids. He'll tell me the truth."

"Okay." The sheriff called out Jaramillo's name and asked the deputy to join him.

Jaramillo walked back to the cell, wide eyed and tentative.

"Gilbert, is it true?" asked Salazar. "Did the Don evict my family from the estate?"

He nodded. "Yes, Eduardo. I'm sorry. Your wife came by a few minutes ago and told us. Don Fernando wants your family off the estate today. His people are packing up your things now."

Salazar slumped onto the bench in his cell and covered his face with his hands.

He was silent for a long moment. Then he looked up at Rivera. "I wish you'd never have come to Rio Arriba County. I asked Josefina to use her witchcraft to drive you away. I even fired a shot at you, hoping to frighten you, hoping you would decide to go back to Utah. I thought that incident with Angie was over with and forgotten. I was trying to protect the Dominguez family. That was my job."

"You didn't kill Angie Pacheco, did you?" asked Rivera.

"My loyalty to the Don ended when he evicted my family from the estate, so now I'll tell you the whole truth. A man who lived on the estate back then came to me one day. He was troubled and frightened. He said he'd been secretly carrying on with Angie Pacheco and that he'd gotten her pregnant. He said he'd just met with her at the bluff by the old *morada* to talk about things. He had no interest in marrying her. He had big plans for his life. He was twenty-five years old, way too old for the Pacheco girl. He had just graduated from law school and had an interest in politics. She told him she would have the child whether he married her or not. He could see his whole future going up in smoke. He panicked and shoved her over the cliff. When he told me about it, he was all shaken up. Babbling like a child. I told him not to worry, I'd check and make sure he was in the clear. I talked to Flaco and learned those three young men were at the old *morada* that day. They were the only potential witnesses. I figured if I eliminated them, he'd be in the clear. I think you know the rest of the story."

"Who was this man?" asked Rivera.

Salazar took a deep breath and let it out. "Alberto Dominguez. The Don's son."

Rivera glanced at the sheriff who appeared shaken and aghast. Rivera looked back at Salazar. "Why would you commit murder for him?"

"It was my job to protect the Don and his family. I was honor bound to do it."

"Honor bound to commit murder?"

"Yes, even that." He raised his chin and produced a haughty expression. "I guess you're not familiar with the concept of total loyalty."

As soon as Salazar had uttered those words, a look of realization came to his face. It seemed to be dawning on him that the Don's loyalty to him had its limits. There was nothing total about it. Salazar sat down and leaned back against the cell wall. "I guess I've been a damn fool."

"One more question," said Rivera. "How did Alberto get from the Dominguez estate to the bluff where Angie was waiting? Wasn't he afraid someone would see him?"

"He didn't use his vehicle. He went through the woods on foot. The old *morada* was only about four miles from the estate."

The sheriff looked at Rivera. "Alberto Dominguez is a very important man in New Mexico politics. He's a state senator and recently announced plans to run for lieutenant governor. This is way above my pay grade. I'm going to notify the state police and the attorney general right away."

33

AFTER A QUICK Mexican plate at Pete's Deluxe Dining Room, Rivera returned to his motel room to relax—his job was done. David Archuleta's killer had been identified and apprehended. Rivera sat down at his desk and began making notes to himself about the case in preparation for writing his report when he returned to Moab. What had started out looking like an owl poaching case soon transformed itself into an illegal drug case. The drug operation intersected in time and place with the murder of a young girl who was killed to protect the reputation of a man with political aspirations. Rivera wished he could be there when the authorities handcuffed Alberto Dominguez. How unfortunate that a lowlife like Dominguez had risen to such high levels in government and might even have become lieutenant governor of the state.

Rivera's thoughts turned to Archuleta and his friend Juan Baeza. Their deaths had been totally unnecessary. Eduardo Salazar had killed them even though they'd never actually witnessed Alberto Dominguez shoving

Angie Pacheco over the cliff. In so doing, Salazar had destroyed three lives—his own and those of two fine young men. Rivera was happy that Victor Sanchez, at least, would be able to come home safely.

Rivera wondered about Don Fernando and how he would react to learning that his son was a murderer just like Salazar. By now he'd have gotten the news. Would he reject his own son the same way he'd rejected Salazar? The Don was wealthy beyond anyone's wildest dreams, but he seemed like an unhappy soul. Presiding over the estate and protecting it all these years must have taken a toll on him. In a way, he was a victim too—a victim of the Dominguez family values which had been passed down over the centuries. Rivera was sure of one thing—despite the perks, he wouldn't want that kind of life.

He didn't know the history of how Dominguez's ancestors had acquired such a large land grant or how they'd managed to keep it intact. Perhaps it had all been accomplished in a legitimate way. Even so, the families in Santa Elena whose land had been stolen from them by unscrupulous men seemed to lead much happier lives than Don Fernando, despite his wealth. The villagers had limited material goods, far less than the Don, but they had a contentment which seemed to derive from family, friends in the community, ancestors buried nearby, a beautiful village to live in, and their religious beliefs and traditions. And they weren't obsessed with careers. They worked with their hands to provide for their families.

Rivera reflected on their history. Their land had been taken from them unjustly. They hoped their land would someday be returned to them—someday they might even fight for it—but despite that longing and despite feeling their ancestors had been cheated, they still seemed to have a certain day-to-day happiness about them. It was as though they'd simply made a decision to be happy regardless of their circumstances. *Happiness is a tricky thing*, Rivera's grandfather had often told him. It was his way of saying that pursuing wealth beyond one's needs was not the path to happiness. Often the reverse was true.

He called Leroy Bradshaw and gave him the news. Bradshaw was relieved the one case he was unable to solve was now closed. He congratulated Rivera and thanked him.

Rivera took the last can of beer out of the refrigerator, popped it open, and took a long swig. He was tired after a long week but felt a deep sense of satisfaction. He decided to call Amy and share the news. He would enjoy telling her the sequence of events that led to his identifying the killer and the importance of the psilocybin mushroom clue she gave him. He dialed her number.

"Hi, Amy. Guess what? The case down here is solved. I'm coming home tomorrow."

"Oh, Manny, I was just getting ready to call you. I have some great news." She sounded excited. "I just received an offer from the University of Hawaii for an Assistant Professor position. I can't believe it. They have one of the most prestigious biology programs in the world. Isn't that exciting?"

Rivera was stunned. "I thought you were planning to go to Albuquerque."

"I was, but then I received this offer."

"So you're going to accept it?"

"Oh Manny, don't you see? This is a dream job. It'll be such a boost for my career. I *have* to accept it."

Rivera felt a numbness of spirit. He said nothing.

"Come with me to Hawaii, Manny. Please come with me."

34

EARLY THE NEXT morning, Deputy Sheriff Manny Rivera checked out of the motel and drove back to Santa Elena. He wanted to see the mountain village one last time before returning to Moab. He crested the last hill on the road into the village and began descending into the valley. The sight of the village gave him a warm feeling as memories of the people he'd met there flooded his mind. He'd developed an enormous respect for them and was saddened that he was leaving. He wondered what it was that had gotten him so attached to this community and its residents.

He knew it was something that transcended the beauty of the mountains and the picture-perfect setting of the village. He sensed it had more to do with the value system of the people of Santa Elena. They had a long and troubled history, deep religious beliefs, and a strong sense of community. They worked hard and helped each other out. Neighbors, the church, and the Penitentes all worked for the common good. Those in need received help without having to ask. And the people revered their ancestors. One could pass away in Santa Elena without fear of being forgotten.

He drove slowly down the main street of the village with his window open. The morning was cool and the air fresh and clean. It was early, so the streets were empty. He passed the Baeza residence, the Sanchez residence, the church, and the Archuleta residence. He looked up the hill behind the church and saw the cemetery and the *morada*. He'd only been here a week but he felt like he'd become a part of the community. He reached the end of the street and made a U-turn. On the way back, he saw Rosita and Perrito coming out of the Sanchez home. He stopped when he reached her.

"Good morning, Rosita."

She waved and gave him a big smile. "My Uncle Victor is coming home. I'm so happy."

"That's wonderful news." Rivera choked up and almost couldn't get the words out. This job had its moments of overwhelming satisfaction. "Now you and Perrito will be able to spend a lot of time with him."

He waved goodbye and rolled on down the street and out of Santa Elena. He stopped at the crest of the hill, took one last look back, and then drove on to Tierra Amarilla.

He parked in front of the sheriff's building and entered. The sheriff was in his office, a good sign that his wife was doing better. Gilbert Jaramillo was at his desk talking on the phone; Gloria and Ruby hadn't arrived yet. He walked into the sheriff's office.

"I'm heading back today. I just stopped in to say goodbye."

Sheriff Gallegos stood up, came around his desk, and shook Rivera's hand. "Thanks for coming down. I couldn't begin to tell you how much I appreciate it."

"It's been a real pleasure working with you," said Rivera. "Have you had any feedback on what's happening with Alberto Dominguez?"

"I got a call from a friend in Santa Fe who works for the state police. They've placed Alberto under arrest. His lawyer is trying to negotiate bail as we speak. The word is already out that Alberto has dropped plans to run for lieutenant governor. No doubt his career as a state senator is finished."

"I wonder how Don Fernando is taking all this."

"Jaramillo visited him last night and filled him in on what Eduardo Salazar had told us. You'll never guess what the Don said."

"What did he say?"

"He was hard as nails. He said, 'If my son has murdered, he should be punished.'"

Rivera shook his head. "At least he's consistent."

"After he said that, he looked very sad according to Jaramillo. He said, 'I can't believe my son would kill my unborn grandchild.'"

"From everything I've heard, the Don loved his grandkids more than anything."

"Listen Manny, as soon as I'm officially sheriff — that'll be in a few months—my first action here will be to offer you a job as my chief deputy. We need you here. I know you love Moab but you could learn to love Rio Arriba County too. What do you think?"

"Well, thank you, Sheriff. I'll give that a lot of thought. You take care and I hope your wife gets better soon." He shook Gallego's hand again and left his office.

On the way out, Deputy Sheriff Gilbert Jaramillo intercepted him. He extended his hand. Rivera shook hands with him and said goodbye. "I learned a lot from you," said Jaramillo.

Just outside the building, Rivera ran into Deputy Sheriff Gloria Valdez who was getting out of her vehicle.

"Manny, are you leaving us?" There was genuine sadness in her voice.

"I'm heading back today. I've enjoyed working with you. You're a good cop." He reached out to shake her hand.

She pushed his hand aside and came in for a hug. She held him tightly and lingered for a long moment. "I'm going to miss you."

"I'm sure I'll be back here again. I'll call you before I come."

"You promise?"

"I promise."

Rivera hopped into his vehicle, waved goodbye to Gloria, and headed north. He was sad to be leaving. He would be back though, after he arranged for David Archuleta's remains to be exhumed and returned to his family. He intended to be in Santa Elena for the reburial and to give Mrs. Archuleta her son's journal.

His experiences in Santa Elena had taught him a lot about life and the importance of family and community. At thirty-six years of age, he wasn't getting any younger. The years were ticking by and still he was without his own family. He was numb at the thought of Amy moving to Hawaii. They'd agreed to talk about it some more after he returned to Moab.

As he headed north to Chama, he decided to take a day off and try to relax. He stopped in Chama and bought a round trip ticket for the Cumbres and Toltec narrow gauge railroad trip to Antonito, Colorado.

Thirty minutes after he boarded the train, it pulled out of Chama and headed north. There were only a handful of people on board, a fact he attributed to the chilly mountain air. He was the only passenger in his car.

After an hour of listening to the rhythmic clicking of the wheels on the rails, he began to relax. The train was passing through a broad treeless valley surrounded by ponderosa pine hills. In the distance, he could see a herd of elk grazing on the grass. It reminded him of the valley in which Santa Elena was nestled, except there were no houses.

He was on the remote borderland between New Mexico and Colorado. To him it was a culturally unique region, a place where land grants, Zapatistas, Penitentes, witches, spells, *curanderas*, owl feathers, and *La Santa Muerte* devotees were part of the fabric of the community. The people were happy despite their poverty. He'd just scratched the cultural surface of this part of the world but he felt a craving to experience more of it.

He'd always wanted to take this train trip with Amy but that was not to be. He knew in his heart that when he returned to Moab, they would talk and hug and there would be tears. But he also knew their relationship was coming to an end. Amy's professional career was important to her and his love of the high country in the Four Corners area was something he could never give up. If he followed her to Hawaii, in a few years other opportunities would arise that might further her career. A high-level appointment in Washington at the Department of the Interior, perhaps. Or some prestigious international assignment at the United Nations. Amy would want to follow those opportunities. That wasn't the kind of life he wanted. He loved her and she him but in his heart, he knew it was over. He guessed he'd always known it would end this way.

Rivera looked out the window. The train was crossing over a trestle spanning a clear creek which tumbled through a rocky chasm. He pictured the creek running to the far side of the valley, joining with other tributaries, becoming part of the Chama River, and from there feeding into the Rio Grande and flowing all the way to the Gulf of Mexico. The water under the trestle was destined for many changes during the course of its existence, just like his own life. In four years, he would be forty; in fourteen years, fifty. He began to feel a sense of time running out.

He knew he needed to make some firm decisions about his life instead of leading a day-to-day existence and then waking up at age sixty and wondering where all the time went. He could remain in Moab and run for sheriff—that would be the right thing for the community. He could go to work for Leroy Bradshaw in Santa Fe—that would reconnect him with his mentor. Or, he could go to work for Sheriff Gallegos in Rio Arriba County and learn more about that fascinating part of the country—that would put him close to Santa Elena and Gloria Valdez. There were other possibilities as well. He knew what his grandfather would tell him: Follow your interests and your heart. That thought triggered a decision—Rivera would take some vacation time, visit his family in Las Cruces, and spend a day with his grandfather. He would talk things through with him and hopefully come up with the right plan for his life.

Author's Note

THE VILLAGE OF Santa Elena, though based upon many of the wonderful villages I've visited in northern New Mexico, is fictional. Likewise, the inhabitants with whom I've populated it are also fictional.

As I've done in all my stories, I've tried to be true to the geography of the area about which I'm writing. However, the Carlo Dominguez land grant and its location, though patterned after the original Tierra Amarilla land grant, are figments of my imagination.

I've also taken some liberties with the schedule of the Cumbres and Toltec narrow gauge railroad. After shutting down for the winter, its summer schedule doesn't begin until late May. I highly recommend the trip—it runs between Chama, NM and Antonito, CO, some of the prettiest mountain country in the United States.

I've found the history and culture of the small villages of northern New Mexico (as well as the Southwest in general) enormously interesting. For those readers wishing to learn more about the area, I'd recommend the following books:

Properties of Violence, by David Correia

Penitente Renaissance, by Ruben E. Archuleta

Trespassers on Our Own Land, by Mike Scarborough

Land of the Penitentes, Land of Tradition, by Ruben E. Archuleta

Rio Arriba, A New Mexico County, by Robert J. Tórrez and Robert Trapp

Blood and Thunder, by Hampton Sides

Valley of the Shining Stone, by Lesley Poling-Kempes

Made in the USA
Middletown, DE
22 October 2023

41207128R00177